Good Girls Shouldn't...

About the author:

Veena S. Halai was born in London and is a graduate of the University of Portsmouth. She is currently working on her next book.

Veena S. Halai

Good Girls Shouldn't...

BLACKAMBER
LONDON

Arcadia Books Ltd
15-16 Nassau Street
London W1W 7AB

www.blackamber.com

Published by BlackAmber
an imprint of Arcadia Books 2006

A catalogue record for this book is available from the British Library.

ISBN 1-901969-26-6

Typeset in Bembo by Basement Press, London
Printed and bound in Finland by WS Bookwell

Arcadia Books gratefully acknowledges the financial support of Arts Council England.

Arcadia Books supports PEN, the fellowship of writers who work together to promote literature and its understanding. English PEN upholds writers' freedoms in Britain and around the world, challenging political and cultural limits on free expression.
To find out more, visit www.englishpen.org or contact
English PEN, 6-8 Amwell Street, London EC1R 1UQ

Arcadia Books distributors are as follows:

in the UK and elsewhere in Europe:
Turnaround Publishers Services
Unit 3, Olympia Trading Estate
Coburg Road London N22 6TZ

in the USA and Canada:
Consortium Book Sales and Distribution
1045 Westgate Drive St Paul, MN 55114-1065

in Australia:
Tower Books
PO Box 213 Brookvale, NSW 2100

in New Zealand:
Addenda
Box 78224 Grey Lynn Auckland

in South Africa:
Quartet Sales and Marketing
PO Box 1218 Northcliffe Johannesburg 2115

Arcadia Books: *Sunday Times* Small Publisher of the Year 2002/03

Acknowledgements

My sincere gratitude to Gary Pulsifer, Daniela de Groote, Rosemarie Hudson and the indispensable team at Arcadia Books for their hard work in turning my loose sheets of paper filled with words into a book which brings my story to life.

In particular, thank you to my editor Joan Deitch for adding her magic touch and last but not least, I would like to thank my family for all their support and encouragement.

For my sisters – Raj, Arti, Neeta and Poonam

1
It's an Asian Thing

*Fujk hbsc uvuf jfyws hkprm oshalitz zweibusc tiheron hba...*confused?
Well, at least now you can understand the way I'm feeling at this
present moment in time. In addition to this baffled state, I have
also entered suicidal mode - which is the result of having no job,
no man and basically no life!

Let's tackle the 'no job' bit first, shall we? I, Nina Nayak, aged
twenty-four, 7 Belgrade Grove, Maida Vale, London, living
under the parental roof (worst luck), am still searching for the
'perfect role that requires the use of my potentially world-
dominating talents'. In other words, dear reader, I am
unemployed.

However, I have absolutely no qualms, nor am I in the least
bit embarrassed about reclaiming the financial gifts that I so
generously gave to the government when I was working for the
past God knows how many months. Nor do I put myself in the
'no job, no hope, on-the-dole person' category just yet. No way!
Nina Nayak is destined for bigger and better things. They just
haven't come her way yet, that's all.

When I have to queue up at the Job Centre so those lucky
people can have my autograph, I always take a look around and
believe me, I am nothing like the other men and women there.

The men, for some bizarre reason, come dressed in their best suits, or designer gear (more commonly known to the fashion police as faux designer gear) just to collect their cheques, which makes me wet myself laughing. Oh well, at least they are not harming anyone else in the process. On the other hand, the women who enter the Job Centre appear to make a day trip of it with their gazillion bawling babies and rampaging toddlers who just end up giving the rest of us a goddamn headache.

I have opted out of queuing up at my local post office to collect this one measly bit of paper around which my poor life seems to revolve. The number of dinosaurs who go in at the same time to harvest their state pension…put it this way, I would be lucky if I got my dosh just before closing time. Anyway, why make more work for myself? Thanks to direct debit, the cash goes straight into my account and I don't even have to get my phat arse out of the door. Phat, by the way means pretty hot and tempting – that's for all you slow movers who felt absolutely ridiculous asking someone what the hell that meant, or just thought I was dyslexic and mis-spelled fat!

Now that we have established that I am unemployed, the saga shall continue. Where was I? Right – I am a young Asian woman who looks like a *Baywatch* babe…hang on, that's a blatant lie as I'm just not tall enough. Since I live in London and attended the local Mountview primary school and The Vale secondary school, I have been fortunate enough to acquire the best of both traditions, Asian and British. That means being able to booze at any hour of the day or night, (although it is more acceptable when the football is on) arising from the English culture, and of course being able to handle my hot 'n' spicy curries – the roots of my Indian inheritance. What a great combination! It turned out to be an ideal preparation for university.

Speaking of which, I graduated a couple of years ago, in Criminology and Legal Studies – no help there, then. In fact, all that mind-behaviour analysis only resulted in paranoia because at one stage I thought I might be suffering from some, if not all, of the mental disorders that contribute to the abnormality of the criminal mind.

Detecting deception was great. Thanks to being exposed to the different methods used by criminologists and the police for sniffing out liars, I am pleased to claim that by following the lecturer's teachings, if I ever did something I should not have done (who, me? Never, Your Honour!), I would have absolutely no problem lying through my teeth. I always knew this skill would come in handy some day. Yeah, like the day I had to go back to my parents' home to become Cindernina, learning how to cook, clean and be a good housewife for my husband-to-be. Honestly, it's like feminism never even existed.

Looking back, I can see what happened to me at uni so clearly now. It went something like this: other irrelevant modules covered in the degree course were taking up far too much space in my brain, so I put them in storage - shovelled them into my unconscious mind. Now for the scientific explanation: whilst the information I wished to retain was making its journey into my brain, it kept coming up against the alcoholic chemicals that were attempting to escape (to all you normal peeps that means sobering up) *out* of my brain after a good night out. This led naturally enough to a collision or a jumbo headache, *resulting in the loss of information*. In the circumstances, I had to ask myself: was there really any point in going to these lectures? They were literally doing my head in. I decided it was essential to stay in bed whenever I felt weak and hung-over. As the days went by, the frequency of bedrest increased...but of course the intention to go to my lectures was always there. And as we all know it's the thought that counts.

According to the impression I gave my mother and father, the four years at university were spent working my arse off to obtain my degree. And as I didn't want to risk my four years of liberty being cut short, I stuck to that line. After all, they were already disappointed that their daughter was not studying for the more respectable career path of law, medicine or accountancy. Simply for this reason, I was the black sheep in the family. Hah! That black sheep would have been dead mutton if they had caught a snapshot of my real persona.

The new me was heavily influenced by my five housemates, two of whom happened to be male. For parental purposes Paul and Chris were referred to as Paula and Christina; they would crop up in conversation whenever I complained to my parents about how they left all the housecleaning for the rest of us, while they buggered off home for most of the weekends. Out of sympathy, my mother said that one weekend she would come and clean the house for us. Oh my God! That would have been disastrous. After that, there were no more complaints about household chores.

My parents, Mr and Mrs Nayak, are very traditional and have set ideas about what girls should be doing and what they definitely *shouldn't*. They are stuck in a time warp; indeed, the new millennium has had absolutely zero effect on them. They have trouble identifying and accepting modern technology, so they end up turning a blind eye to it. This attitude is reflected in their approach to me and my sister Vanessa, and to anyone else under the age of ninety. They still don't get the fact that *ALL* youngsters have a few drinks (we're not talking 7UP here) and that social networking is sparked off in bars and other watering-holes, even though water has nothing to do with it. Going out with your mates to bars and clubs is the best way to make more friends – and meet potential lovers! That's part of the British lifestyle, isn't it? Or should I say 'innit'?

Well anyhow, it is forbidden for their good little Indian girls to go clubbing. My parents obviously don't go to The Ministry of Sound or Equinox themselves so they have no idea what it's all about. Instead, they have formed a sinister image of the clubbing scene, confirmed when channel-flicking on our ancient TV where they come across one of those manky 'club-uncovered' programmes set in Falaraki, or closer to home, in Liverpool or Newcastle. When this happens, I make it my duty to grab the remote control and change channels, relieved that my cover hasn't yet been blown, or hoping that, if I *was* at the scene, that the stupid cameraman didn't catch a glimpse of me slumped in the corner being sick or cavorting with men in compromising situations.

I've actually become a pro at dodging production crews who decide to film a television documentary on the same night that I am out clubbing. All my friends are jumping around to make visible any part of their bodies on the TV screen while I, on the other hand, sneak away, trying to make myself invisible...and after a few drinky-winkies, it's not that difficult for me to actually believe that I am.

My parents don't want me to be associated with the other tarts who wear belts as skirts and dance around in a drunken and disorderly state (say no more)! And...er...having a bit of harmless fun with the opposite sex is *definitely* a no-no. It should never be indulged in by any good little Indian girl. And just in case you were wondering, that good little Indian girl is me.

The funny thing is that when it's someone else's daughter or son behaving in that fashion, my parents don't overreact, but as soon as it comes to their own offspring, it's a totally different story. In our middle-class Hindu culture, the fear of what other people might say heavily moulds the way in which we behave. Peeping Toms have nothing better to do than to sit by their squeaky clean windows and spy on what other households are up to. They go on to give a detailed report, when they have one of their mothers' meetings, even though they always get the wrong end of the stick. Little do they know that it is usually their own son or daughter who is at the top of the slappers league table. I guess you just have to learn to ignore those people who thrive on gossip. They are nothing but a waste of space.

My parents immigrated to London in the 1970s, in flight from Uganda during the Idi Amin regime. It must have been a difficult time for them, having lost nearly everything but their lives, to adapt to the British lifestyle, find work and have a family. Before my mother had me, she worked as a receptionist for a small Latin-American company. My father was employed in the building trade. He routinely changed jobs, due to the indiscreet racial abuse that was hurled at him by people who supported the BNP. This treatment naturally made them very insular and so British culture has had very little influence on them. They have kept to their Indian traditions and made sure these were passed on to me and my younger sister, Vanessa. As the Asian population expanded, the community became close-knit and people helped each other in times of trouble, so that's another reason why Mum and Dad are so behind the times.

Our house in sunny north-west London is a typical Asian home. The through-lounge has cream leather sofas at one end and a wooden dining table covered with a plastic sheet to prevent it from looking old and shabby, at the other. A glass cabinet packed with medals and trophies, mixed in with a few family photos, takes up most of the space and makes the room look smaller. The walls are hung with illustrated copper plates and there are lots of African knick-knacks. There is also a vase full of tacky plastic flowers that I keep hiding away but which miraculously keeps reappearing in full view where my mother had originally placed it. The house is kept in immaculate condition, including two out of the three bedrooms. Mine is the exception.

My younger sister, Vanessa, has acquired my mother's genes. She also suffers from that obsessive-compulsive disorder for cleanliness. That is one of the reasons why we used to fight like cat and dog. When we were younger, we would chase each other around the dining table shouting and screaming. The ultimate objective was to beat each other up, but soon enough it had become a game of cat and mouse and we had forgotten about our initial disagreement. Sadly, even when we did manage to play together, we would always end up fighting. Okay, in most of these circumstances I admit that it was my fault, I always took the game that little bit too far. I would ignore Vanessa's demands to stop tickling her, until her laughter turned into tears. Sometimes she would wet her pants because she was laughing so much, which then resulted in anger, and the whole commotion would start all over again.

Vanessa is very different from me. Her life is so organised that she cannot cope with any unexpected issues that arise. Everything has to be pre-planned, especially when it comes to revising for her exams. Somewhere in her 'plan for the day' she probably has certain times to visit the toilet. When I was studying for my A levels, I was never at home either. The difference was that she goes to the library to revise while I was in the pub with friends supposedly doing the same thing!

I swear my sister has a Jekyll and Hyde personality. When she is out with her friends she does not care about anything or anyone. She has no concept of time and these days she is never at home. Aspiring to be a doctor at the age of eighteen, she was already in my father's good books. However, we became much closer when I went off to university for those four years. I know she would never admit to it, but I think my not-so-little sister missed me when I was away. These days, we have set aside our differences and chosen to stick together whenever our parents start to stress us out.

However, sometimes she would take charge and say, 'When I go off to med. school, not only are you going to miss me, but you'll be begging me to introduce you to all the George

Clooneys that I end up working with in real life ER'. She was absolutely right – after all, who would miss out on an opportunity like that? Definitely not me!

2
The Snip Trip

Even A-list celebrities have the odd 'bad hair day', but when you compare that to what the rest of us unworthy humans suffer from - a bad hair decade - I guess it's pretty good.

Recently, I had decided that I couldn't be bothered with all the added stress of taking hours to untangle my waist-length dark brown hair, and make it look all pretty. You see, at the back of my mind I knew that no matter how much gel, mousse and hairspray I used, the 'lovely' British weather would totally exasperate me. The rain would flatten my style and make my hair look greasy, and just when I thought it couldn't get any worse, the wind would blow the wet strands all over my face. Grrreat! I had experienced this one too many times and now I was sick of it. The time had definitely come for a change.

After weighing up the pros and cons, I opted to spend my fortnight's dole money on a top hairdresser, hoping that my new style would uplift my dreadful week, even though my past experiences with hairdressers have been unsuccessful to say the least. Is it just me or does everyone have problems with their hairstylist?

Every time I enter a salon, I explain to the hair doctor exactly what I would like done to my hair. Sometimes I even take along a picture, cut out of a magazine. It's not my fault they don't understand my detailed description...so it is easier to show them. Usually it's pretty straightforward - a simple cut with a few feathery bits at the front. Now that's not very complicated, is it? All I can say is that most hairdressers who have been anywhere near my hair would have difficulty understanding *The Idiot's Guide to Hairdressing*. How can they get it so wrong? Even someone with visual and auditory impairment could do a better job. And why do I always get the least experienced one? The one who has no clue about hair whatsoever?

Over the years, I have noticed that, while in the salon, I always agree to liking my horrible haircut. Why is this? I think these people must use hypnotic powers to convince us that our hair actually looks decent. I always end up falling for this and stupidly believe it - that is until I step back out into the 'real world' where everything looks dull and grey, just like my crappy haircut. At this point, I usually tie it up in a ponytail and go shopping for a hat, cap, bandanna or anything that will cover my head.

This time I was taking no chances. I didn't want a dud hairdo, especially since I intended to have it cut drastically short and knew that my parents would have something to say, like: what the f**k have you done to your hair! No doubt a fear of me being a lezzie would immediately run through their minds, but this obviously won't be mentioned aloud, because just like shags, drugs and drink, this is also a taboo subject for Asian families. I thought maybe I should get the hairdresser to put in some colour while she was at it, just to add a few more sparks to the fireworks that would go off at home tonight. Hmm. It was going to be an interesting day, especially if I ended up hating my new cut.

I made my way to the bus stop, dreading my forty-minute journey. Public transport in London is a nightmare. I can just about bear the forty minutes, but it's the waiting for the bus to get its arse into gear and arrive on time that kills me. I'm sure that 99 per cent of bus users will vouch for the fact that waiting for a bus adds an extra hour to the trip – and don't be fooled, that's just on the way there: you've still got the return journey to look forward to. The remaining 1 per cent who disagree are most likely to be bus drivers, or even bus spotters, if they exist.

I need to have a quick rant about buses here. Please turn over the page if you use your own car or live in some civilised part of the country like Bognor Regis or Halifax, where I bet these little beauties run on time. London is famous for its double-decker red buses, even though the only people who use them in chock-a-block Central London are tourists who have all the time in the world. London buses have built up such a proud reputation for unreliability, invisibility even, that commuters would rather suffer the pungent smell of other people's BO or other gaseous compounds sneakily released from their backsides on the heavily packed tube trains, just to get to work on time. If you were out in the cold, waiting and waiting and waiting – *and waiting* – I have a feeling you would too. But sadly sometimes buses are the cheaper and more geographically convenient mode of transport.

At the bus stop, I stood alone, whiling away the time by testing my eyesight on car registration plates at certain distances and playing a little game that keeps me amused for a while. Every car that zooms past, I give the driver a rating ranging from 'butt ugly' to 'drop dead gorge'. Although ratings tend to stay at the 'butt ugly' end of the scale, by the time boredom kicks in, I can usually see the bus from afar.

Not today, however. I had done my fill of judging and there wasn't a bus in sight. Not even one going the opposite way. Now I know this may seem strange, but it brings extra hope, as logically if a bus goes past in the opposite direction then it or another bus should eventually arrive, going back the other way. That's the theory, anyway.

As I stood there, hunched against the wind, an old red Ford Cortina came jolting along the road and drew up nearby. I kept myself occupied by rereading the billboards and the bus timetable. Out of the corner of my eye I could see a revolting man leaning out of the window. He looked pretty much like Saddam Hussein's long lost brother. With a major lisp, he said, 'ello baybee, you whanth to coma fora rythe?' Urghhh! Although I wanted to give him a piece of my mind, I didn't want to provoke him. What if he really was Saddam's brother, and he had a gun? I tried to peer surreptitiously through the back window of his car to see if he had kidnapped anyone else along the way. My heart was beating so fast that if he had tried to get out of the car, I would have died of a heart attack on the spot. Then hallelujah! I saw the bus turning into the road and thought to myself, if he says anything else then I'm giving as good as I get. He started laughing and added, 'Eh tsweethi, you wantha tscrew?' and just before I had the chance to retaliate by shouting 'Go tscrew yourra mama,' traffic started moving and the stupid prick sped off. Thank God! This is all part and parcel of the London Bus Ordeal.

When I got on, I deliberately sat at the back of the bus. I couldn't be dealing with all the stress of feeling obliged to give up my seat halfway into the journey for some OAP, who didn't even look that old and who might just take my seat and not even utter a word of thanks. I swear some of them take it for granted. They usually hover about at the front, waiting for someone to offer them a seat. To avoid this, the best thing to do is to sit at the back. It works every time as the lazy old gits won't venture that far.

The driver was Speedy Gonzales. He must have been running really late, so thanks to him, my journey was a lot quicker than expected. Instead of forty minutes, the roller-coaster ride took a mere twenty-five. If seatbelts had been provided it might not have been such a life-threatening experience. Nevertheless, at least now I wouldn't be late for my appointment, I thought smugly, getting off and feeling glad to be still in one piece. That was until I looked around and realised, to my dismay, that I had got off a good half-mile too soon.

In case you don't know it, haven't even heard of it maybe, Edgware Road is interesting firstly for the fact that there is no 'e' in the edge bit. You can always tell out-of-towners because they spell it Edgeware. Secondly, the road is a winding thoroughfare, several miles long. It goes from Marble Arch (posh houses, Lebanese restaurants, glittering casinos, Oriental carpet shops and hookah-joints) to Maida Vale (swanky apartments, posh houseboats, retired actors and tree-lined avenues) to Kilburn (Primark, street markets, Irish butchers and live-music pubs) to Cricklewood (Bingo halls, refugees, fish and chip shops and *White Teeth* territory).

Like a magical mystery tour, my bus passed through all these very different areas. Dilemma! Here I was, at the Kilburn part, needing to get further down towards Marble Arch. Should I redo the 'waiting for a London bus' thing? No! These boots were made for walking.

After a twenty-two-minute brisk march, my legs felt like jelly and I could hardly breathe. I know what you're thinking, but let me assure you that I'm fit as a fiddle. A little stroll like that would be my warm-up exercise when I'm at the gym. All right - for argument's sake let's blame my state of collapse on the weather and the pollution.

The Gino Bertelli salon was small, but very plush. I almost fell in the door and the receptionist stared at me as though I was from the planet Mars. I had forgotten how awful and sweaty I must be looking.

'Can I help?' she uttered, obviously hoping that the answer would be, 'no'.

'Hi, I've got an appointment - my name is Nina.' Miss Snooty told me to take a seat. In front of me was a pile of

13

magazines. I would have liked to have glanced through them in case I found a better style than that which I had in mind. Unfortunately, I didn't have enough time. I looked up for a brief moment and a young woman waved me over towards her.

I put on the black cape (if I had the mask, I could have been mistaken for Batwoman) and sat on the chair. However, I was damned if the lady who was ruffling her fingers through my hair was also going to be cutting it, as her own hair didn't inspire much confidence. She was an ideal candidate to appear on ITV's *Haircuts from Hell*, if the programme ever existed. Her hair on the left side was at least half a foot longer than the right side and it was dyed in various colours. Basically every colour in the rainbow.

In conversation, I foolishly asked her the million dollar question, and learning that she *had* cut her own hair, I was tempted to kill myself with the scissors there and then and get it over and done with. I then discovered that she was slightly cross-eyed. This must explain why her hair had ended up in such a state, and what she was capable of doing to mine! Oh well, another anecdote to be added to my long list of bad hair experiences…what else was new?

I sat there mortified, lacking the balls to ask for another hairdresser to cut my hair. However, after all that, Ms Rainbow did a fantastic job and I was left feeling really guilty for my negative thoughts. I decided a hefty tip would compensate…and I think it did!

When I came out of the salon, I was feeling really good. Then things got even better. As I was walking back to the bus stop I bumped into an old schoolfriend – someone I used to fancy the pants off. That's a lie, by the way. I still do!

'Kieran!' I cried.

'Hey Neen, ain't seen ya in ages. How you been gal?' I couldn't help wondering why he was using the rude boy lingo, but that was ok as I was concentrating on holding back the urge to pounce on him.

After a bit of small talk and exchange of numbers (*woohoo!*), he noticed my new haircut. 'So you hadda haircut huh? Or is that really all your facial hair?'

Shiiiiiiiiiiiiit!! That stupid cow at the Gino Bertelli salon had forgotten to brush the little snippets of hair off my face! She *so* didn't deserve that tip! I'd half a mind to nip back and get it off her. Dying of embarrassment, I cut the conversation short and dashed to the nearest toilets, which happened to be in McDonald's, and made myself look a little more presentable.

Unsurprisingly, I just missed the next bus and the journey home took longer than ever. Plodding down the street towards my house and all the hassle awaiting me there, I gloomily wondered if I would ever hear from Kieran. I decided not to get my hopes up too much.

Yes, it had been just another bad hair day, after all.

3
Parental Talks

'O Bhagwaan! You look like a boy.' Weeping as well as attempting to shout, my mother continued, 'what boy is going to want to merry another boy?…Just wait till your deddy gets home…'

Blah, blah, blah, blah, blah. I blocked out the rest and went upstairs to reassure myself that I had done a good job and that my dad would get over it too.

That evening there were plenty of sparks; in fact, the firework displays on Guy Fawkes' night or Diwali were damp squibs in comparison. The man of the house was furious. Instead of hearing the words, all I could envisage were flames coming out of his mouth and smoke from his ears. I was already being punished by having to sit through one of his lectures about how this culture had taken over our traditions. I couldn't get a word in edgeways. All I wanted to say was, 'Hey, look, it's a trivial matter. My hair will soon grow back.'

However, he carried on and on and on: 'The whole beauty of the Indian girl is in her long hair…now you look ugly.'

I mentally got the heavy-duty shields out to block that latter insult, and assumed the 'teenage attitude' of taking negative blessings positively. That means when it comes to fashion, always adopting the opposing view to that which has been kindly suggested by the oldies.

'From now on, you are going to do much more to help your ma in the house,'

My dad was droning. 'We already have the problem of finding you a good husband because of your non-existent hair and we don't want them to think that you have no interest in cooking and doing other household chores.'

Why should I have to lie? I *don't* have any interest in those things! Fabulous! This was all I needed, an intensive course on 'being a good housewife'. I could just imagine it:

Part 1 *The Instruments Used to Keep Your Home Immaculate* (Tutor - my mum)
Part 2 *Cooking: 'Let It Be a Second Nature to You* (Tutor - Madhur Jaffrey)
Part 3 *Babies: For a Perfect Indian Family* (Tutor - my gran)

Better start preparing...

My father's grand speech was finally coming to an end. 'I let you go out to study and you come back looking like you belong to the Western culture!'

True, I wanted to rebel. But I didn't think it was the right time to confess that he was partly correct and that I do occasionally: wear the odd short skirt, smoke the odd fag, gulp alcoholic beverages as if there is no tomorrow and share a bed with male friends. Bearing in mind the mood in the household, the consequences would have been fatal. Options considered here would be similar to those that were applied in the Big Brother house:

1. *You have been evicted. Please leave the traditional Indian house.*
2. *You are no longer our daughter. You no longer live in the traditional Indian family.*
3. *You will be rehabilitated in India, where you will learn how to live in the traditional Indian house.*
4. *You're dead - full stop.*

If I had the money I would move out, but living in my dad's house meant abiding by his rules. I was expecting the silent treatment from both of them for at least a couple of days, so I went upstairs, crawled into bed and did my own *Thought for the Day*, trying to judge whether it was time to make an early entrance into hibernation.

The next morning, the world was looking brighter. Things had calmed down after the previous night's explosion. Luckily, I had no plans for the rest of the week as I was under strict orders to help my mother clean the house and was to be kept under supervision in case I did anything stupid again. To the naked eye the house couldn't be any cleaner. But with the duster in sight, my mother kept getting ideas that there were an abundant number of dust-mites that had to be *ex*-ter-min-ated. Vanessa had already left for college. The cheeky cow had left me a little post-it note:

'Your hair looks fab - it was worth getting into trouble for!

Ps. You might as well do my share of the house chores too - that will get you back in their good books! Cheers.'

A TV advertisement suddenly came to mind. You know, the one where the girl spills beer everywhere around the house and her boyfriend licks the place sparkling clean. I would make our house twice as clean just to get my taste-buds on an intoxicating beverage. This is how people start to think when they are in a vulnerable state and deprived of necessities! I would go even further if a fag was on offer, I'd even offer to iron my dad's Damart long johns! How disgusting! This was certainly not healthy thinking.

I started off by vacuuming the upstairs. Not only did our powerful vacuum suck up every speck of dirt and dust, it was so monstrous and hungry it also decided to eat one of my sister's socks that was innocently lying on the floor. Instead of switching off and unplugging the Hoover, opening up the bag and allowing all the dust to escape into thin air, I left the sock in there. When the 'missing sock' drama commences, it will be amusing to see how long the search (conducted by my sister) goes on for and the places where she looks. After all, I don't really have any other entertainment for the moment. As I wended my way into my parents' room, the Hoover had yet again managed to collect a souvenir from the room. I heard my mum's hairpins rattle around in the pipeline before being swallowed into the bag, where they joined Vanessa's sock and before I could stop it, in went dad's discount voucher for Tums indigestion tablets. Little did I know, that more trouble was on its way, and it had my name written all over it...

4
World Turned Upside Down

This is not a mistake – I have deliberately written this page so that the reader has to turn the book upside down. There is a purpose behind this. I thought I would give you the chance to share some of the discomfort I felt when my parents suddenly announced that they had arranged for me to see 'a good Indian boy' and only decided to tell me about it two days prior to the engagement. I meant engagement as in 'meeting', of course – not the 'ring to finger thing'! I would also like to take this opportunity to apologise to some of my friends who have been through this ghastly experience, only to be laughed at by myself when they were telling me how embarrassed and annoyed they were. I now know *exactly* how they felt, and I give them full permission to laugh at me.

Just slightly off the point again: how about reading this bit on the train or bus while going to work? Can you imagine the type of reaction you might get from your fellow passengers when they see you turn the book upside down? If you can't, then why not experiment? You may even be lucky enough to start up a conversation with someone, despite the general consensus that all Brits are reticent. In their own country, perhaps. However, they show no signs of hesitancy when on holiday in Ibiza or Ayia Napa, do they? So why not give it a try? Your worst scenario would be that people think you've gone totally bananas. However, there are always two sides to a coin, so it could also mean that you are a trendsetter for starting conversations with others. (NB: remember to promote my book!)

To revert to the dreaded subject of 'a suitable boy', I still had not come up with a plan to avoid meeting this guy, whose name I didn't even know. For the first time in my life I was clueless. There was no way out of this: I'd have to go and see him. But, if for one minute my parents thought I was going to wear a bloody sari, they could forget the whole thing! I got away with not wearing one for my cousin's wedding, and instead wore one of those *shalwar kameez* outfits. To those of you, who don't know, that is the equivalent of a tunic top and baggy MC Hammer bottoms! Anyway I was definitely NOT wearing one for some stupid little boy whom I had never even met. If only I could think of a good excuse to get out of this.

To complicate matters even further, I got a text message from Kieran inviting me to his party on Saturday night. Naturally, I accepted. But nothing in my life is ever straightforward. The problem was, I had to meet Mr Nice Guy the very next morning. Oops!

The Friday evening was spent at home helping my mother cook and clean, for the sole purpose of earning a few extra brownie points before I mentioned to her that I was going out for a social gathering on Saturday. To my surprise, I felt like the timorous lion from *The Wizard of Oz*, who needed courage. Every time I tried to bring up the subject, I stopped, as I wasn't sure how she would react. I couldn't even employ the 'Dutch Courage Rule' because that, of course, involved alcohol. So the only approach was to just tell her that I was going.

21

Lo and behold, despite my trepidation, she was fine about it. These parental people work in aberrant ways. Maybe I had done a really ace job with the cleaning and cooking. Or it could have been that she had pinned her hopes on me getting hitched in the very near future and therefore didn't want to put me in a humongous strop and ruin my chances on Sunday. Gaining courage, I decided to push my luck and suggested staying over at a friend's house, because of course it would be too late to come back home by myself. Yet again, after a little hesitation she agreed, but made it very clear that if I was not home by nine o'clock on Sunday morning, my life would not be worth living.

Mission accomplished, I had no time to procrastinate. Usually it takes me more than one day to plan what to wear and sort out what to do with my hair for a big night out. But luckily, I only needed to plan my outfit, because there was not much that could be done with my hair, now it was so short.

My first task was to phone the Queen of Clubs, Alisha, who also happens to be my best friend since the age of six, ex-uni housemate and my unofficially adopted sister. I wanted to know if she was going to the party. As ever, she didn't disappoint me. After discussing the usual 'what to wear, hair, who else would be there', I went to try on a few dozen outfits, narrowed it down to the best three and concluded that the matter was better left to dwell upon.

Yawning, I got into bed and in a childlike manner, tightly closed my eyes, so tomorrow would come much quicker. Various thoughts were hampering my efforts to reach the Land of Nod. Feeling restless, I got out of bed and finally decided on what I should wear 'to the ball', and more importantly, how I would impress Kieran. I then dived back into my bed. The one thing I would definitely find out at the party was whether he had a girlfriend.

I had just entered stage 2 of the sleep cycle when some moron sent a text message to my phone and woke me up. It was

Kieran, persuading me to go to his party. I was ready to text back, but my evil side got the better of me. I decided to keep him in suspense and went back to sleep.

The next morning, I replied to the text message from the night before and was ready to go round to Alisha's house. We spent the day doing girlie stuff, which consisted of painting our nails, applying facemasks and catching up on gossip. Time elapsed quickly and the hour soon arrived to make our way to the party. I had decided to wear black trousers to complement my revealing mauve-coloured crochet top. Ally stuck to all black; she once read in a magazine that wearing black clothes makes people look dramatically thinner, so I left her to it.

Very sensibly and maturely, as was right for my age, I promised myself that due to the shenanigans occurring tomorrow, I would either control my alcoholic intake, or resist the temptation altogether. Realistically, however, there was no way I was going to hold back at a party. Yes, I was going to get well and truly shitfaced.

When we arrived at the party, the furniture had been kept to the bare minimum, which gave the illusion that the house was enormous. Kieran looked gorgeous. His mysterious green eyes were already glazed over; he welcomed us in and directed us straight to the bar. He must have read my mind!

Within five minutes of arriving, Ally and I had already drunk four glasses of Archers and lemonade between us. Well, I had downed three while she was still on her first. Disappointed that they were not having an immediate effect, I moved on to the Sambuca.

There weren't many girls at the party, which was a good thing, but those who were there had a major attitude problem with us; they were probably scared that, as the only Asian chicks, we would hog the limelight and get all the attention from the boys. I like to look at it as healthy competition myself. If looks could kill, then Ally and I would have been on the floor in a shot. But that didn't stop us from socialising and flirting with the boys in the room and having a good time. That's all I remember! Actually, I also recall playing a few games too, but that's about it.

At 6 am I woke up still pissed as a fart, only to find Ally's bum shoved in my face. My head was spinning and I needed the sick bucket. I was trying to figure out if everything usually floats around in mid-air or whether my eyes were playing tricks on me. God knows whose bed we were sleeping on. Worse still, I couldn't remember how I had got there. My clothes were still intact – was that a good sign or bad? I was suffering from amnesia, and as for the question: Did I accomplish my mission to find out if Kieran had a girlfriend? Well, I wasn't quite sure. I rolled over to get off the bed, and thump!! The top half of my body got to the floor before my legs did. That hurt!

With one sandal still attached to my right foot, not quite sure where the other one had disappeared to, I tiptoed into the bathroom and washed my face. There was a burning sensation on my forehead and I looked in the mirror. That bastard of a carpet burn left a graze on my spam. How was I supposed to cover that? I dabbed a wet tissue over it, but that was no good.

The overpowering smell of half-empty wine bottles, beer cans and strong spirits was not aiding my hangover; in fact it was making it worse because I was starting to think irrationally. I kept imagining that I would be known as the female version of the rap star Nelly, with the slight exception that the trademark of the little white plaster on his cheek would now be on my forehead. Not sure where that thought appeared from: surely a normal person would have seen more of a resemblance to Mr Bump out of the Mr Men collection?

I needed fresh air and a jumbo-sized carton of Toothkind Ribena. As I went to wake up Ally, Kieran stood near the door, kissed me and thanked me for coming. I was left wondering as to whether we did have a snog and a bit of a fumble last night or was that a figment of my imagination? Fortunately, he failed to notice the artwork on my forehead, so he must have still been drunk too. But I didn't have time to think about that now. I had to rush home to prepare for the exciting day ahead of me (yeah right).

I craved *foooood*. I felt weak and needed my bed. I was NEVER drinking again!

We staggered back to Ally's house, where I had a quick shower. Nevertheless I could still smell alcohol and hoped it was only me being paranoid because my mother is an 'alcohol detective'. I was, understandably, not in the mood or in a stable condition to go and see this guy. I also started suffering from the shakes, which is a sign of sleep deprivation - I learnt that in a 'psych' module. The most horrible thing was that this was all self-inflicted.

The hung-over, bad little Indian girl set off for home at 7 am, feeling very sorry for herself. As I was walking back to my house, eating a buttered slice of toast on the way, I couldn't help wondering exactly what had happened last night. The sheer ambiguity of it all was turning up the volume of the drums that were already banging in my head. So I focused on keeping my eyes open, at least while crossing the roads and dodging the shit on the pavement that someone's untrained dog had so inconveniently placed there. Finally I could see my house, but I still had to make my way past the fifty houses before it.

It was still too early on a Sunday morning for cars to be on the roads and people to be awake. Thank God, I had enough time to get home and maybe even snatch forty winks. With a jacket over one arm and a heavy bag firmly gripped in each hand, I struggled to find my keys. Wait a minute…in my rush to get home for that extra hour of sleep I had bloody forgotten the most important bag which not only contained the house keys but potentially my sanity too. I could have sworn that God was punishing me! I would never make it to Ally's house and back again. I already felt weak, I had a graze on my forehead and I was on the verge of passing out.

It was all too much. I stopped in my tracks and sat on the wall. Apart from taking the risk of getting to the front door and trying to open the damn thing by putting my hand through the letterbox and knowing my luck, getting it stuck, there was no other alternative but to go back to get the keys. I wanted to leave the rest of my stuff behind but opted to take it with me. After all, we didn't live in a Neighbourhood Watch area.

My all-round trip took another thirty minutes (it felt like three hours) in order for me to arrive back at the original spot. My feet were numb from the pain of walking in those sandals, my hands were numb from the agony of carrying the bags, since the handles were digging into my palms, and my brain was numb from an alcohol overdose and that unintentional effort to kiss the floor.

Oh no! Our new neighbours from over the road, Flora and Phil were already up and at it, the hyper-active gits. They were out on the pavement, busy unloading lots of strange sculptures from their car into their house. I tried to dodge them by looking down and heading straight for our front door.

Literally dying of dehydration, I unlocked the door, crept inside, dropped my bags and headed straight for the kitchen. After filling my 'thirst tank' with five glasses of water I tiptoed upstairs and jumped into bed. My eyes closed straight away and I felt like I could have slept for a million years. But when does anything ever turn out the way we want it to? All that water meant getting out of bed every twenty minutes and letting the bladder loose. I should have just fallen asleep on the toilet seat. In spite of this, the effects were positive as I started to feel a little better.

Most of the houses on our street are identical to each other. Recently, however, an arty-farty couple moved into the house opposite, and what used to be a perfectly 'normal' house, with a white-painted exterior, is now a shrine to that 1980's children's show *Rainbow*, with Bungle, Zippy and George – remember them? The house has been painted purple with a red door and white window frames. Apparently it is all in the name of modern art. At least now, no one can complain about having problems finding where I live. After all, it is directly opposite the newly renovated *Rainbow House*.

Not long after Flora and Phil had moved into our street, a brief introduction took place while they were attempting to trim the little hedgerow in front of their house and turn it into an animal shape. While I was doing my daily chore of emptying the rubbish into the outside bin, I made an effort to go and see if they had settled into their new home. Flora and Phil are both artists and very much into contemporary art. Their poor house was getting a Laurence Llewellyn-Bowen makeover.

After discovering that I was of Asian descent, they could not stop talking about their expedition to India and how their guru guided them to enlightenment. What complete and utter crap, I thought to myself. It was not the bloody guru showing them this supposed light at the end of the tunnel, it was surely the special herbs that they were experimenting with - and I am not talking about green tea either. It certainly explains their sublime 'lack of concern' and chilled-out mood that is evident whenever we see them. Instead of waving, they just smile and do the peace sign.

Based on what our new neighbours had done to their house, and the fact that it was directly opposite ours, my mother decided that they were completely mad and stupid too, for that matter. My dad was more worried about the value of our property decreasing because of their house. Although stereotypically judgmental about Flora and Phil, my parents were not the type to show their true feelings when they finally did bump into the two hippies. That's what I had thought, anyway.

Then one morning, my mother opened the front door to sign for some post that had been delivered. Flora and Phil were walking by and seeing my mum, decided to greet her in their usual manner. Big mistake. The two fingers went up and my mother was outraged. She read the 'peace sign' as an offensive swear sign and shouted, "You racist!" before slamming the door shut. When the subject arose, I attempted to tell her that it was a case of miscommunication, but she would stop me in my tracks and say that she knew exactly what she saw. Under no circumstances was she going to apologise: she didn't like them anyway.

The corollary to all this is that every time I leave the house, I have to ensure that Flora and Phil are not outside at the same time, in order to avoid the embarrassing situation my mother had got herself into. Unfortunately, trying to avoid and dodge the neighbours is as exciting as it gets for the residents on our street. Even a police car speeding through this suburban road with its flashing blue light would be an historical event for us.

Ally lived only a few streets away, yet she experienced everything but quietness. The road, on which her house was situated had become a short-cut for people who thought they were avoiding the traffic that was building up on the main road. Cars were parked at both sides of this two-way narrow road, and drivers had to take the risk of coming face to face with another car half-way down the road, then having an argument about who should reverse their car to let the other one through. In some cases, stubborn, irate drivers have been known to switch off their engines, and disputes have lasted for as long as half an hour. The little street becomes *really* noisy when the rest of the drivers in the queue roll down their windows and start hurling abuse and beeping their horns.

That's what happens when the capital city has a few too many drivers, all too impatient and too stressed out to bother signalling at roundabouts or even stop at pedestrian crossings. People who wait for a car to stop to let them cross the road don't stand a chance of ever getting to the other side - they should just start walking across and force the vehicles to stop. But if everyone started doing that, there would be a greater number of hit and run incidents. Nothing can stop these maniac drivers, apart from the traffic lights, which have recently incorporated cameras to help catch and punish these assholes.

Okay, I've just had another mini-rant. But what you've got to remember is that I was wrecked, short-haired and in disgrace, half in love with Kieran and wholly in hate with my would-be suitor. It had been a long night, and it sure as hell was going to be a long, long day...

5
Boys - the Indian Version

My mother was surprised to see me in bed with the covers over my head. I'm usually a very light sleeper and always hear her entering my room. Given the circumstances, this time was an exception. In her rush to wake me up she opened the one curtain that I had managed to draw in my lifeless condition and was mumbling something about why the other one was left open. Before she started to pull back the covers and demand that I get up, I told her from underneath my covers that I was awake. Naturally my head was still a little sore and I was feeling queasy.

'Your room looks a mess. Don't think I'm going to pick up all those clothes from your floor,' she nagged. 'When are you going to change your ways, beta?'

Great! A migraine was now emerging on top of my original headache. I was in no fit state to have an argument, or even talk to her for that matter, so I apologised and that finally got her out of the room.

A quarter of an hour later, I got my arse out of bed and went to have another quick shower, hoping that the hot water would make me feel a little more fresh and alive and possibly wash away my hangover too. However, that was asking a bit too much. After making my room look orderly, which meant stuffing all my clothes into a cupboard and promising myself to tidy it up later, I went downstairs to join my mum for breakfast. All I wanted was a cup of tea, as food would not have stayed in my stomach very long. So it was best to avoid brekkie.

'What's wrong with you?' my mother fussed. 'You don't look well.'

'I've got a headache,' I replied weakly.

'It must have been something you ate last night at your friend's house.'

More like something I drank, I wanted to say. Insisting that I should take some medication, Mum was also quick to say that this would not stop us from going to visit the would-be bridegroom that morning. So if it were a little act I was putting on then nothing would come of it. 'Even if you were on your last limbs I would take you there myself,' she finished triumphantly.

Quite ironic really, considering I had been practically legless the night before. I could see I was definitely not getting out of this one.

I wanted to know exactly what I was letting myself in for. The more information I got from my mum, the less I would have to ask this mystery man, which in effect meant that I would have to spend only a small amount of time with him.

'So what's this guy's name?' I said.

'Guy? You don't call someone you don't know a cow!' she stated, looking at me in disgust.

This woman is absolutely mad. All I wanted was a name and now I had to explain to her that I was not being disrespectful. Although a word that sounds like 'guy' may mean 'cow' in Hindi, it is also a slang term for 'man' in the English language. Her long explanation about how I tend to use words from different languages to make up a whole sentence and how that can confuse the listener took up the next few minutes. My eyes

31

began to close. It was not my fault she misunderstood what I was talking about.

Anyway, she suddenly said to me: 'I don't know his name, I don't know his age, I don't know his life story.'

'Yeah, well that gives us something in common - except I don't want to know his name, I don't want to know his age and I'm certainly not interested in his life story.'

Oops! Had I just said that out aloud? I thought so, but she chose to ignore my comments and said that I should go and get ready because apparently it takes me so long. I needed to be comfortable, and thought longingly of joggers, a sweatshirt and trainers. But that would never do. Some dark jeans and a light blue shirt would perfectly express the mood I was in. I added some colour to my face by applying lipstick and eyeliner and then went downstairs to surprise my mum by being ready.

'Where are you going now?' she rapped out.

'I'm ready to go,' I said, puzzled.

'Oh my God! What is wrong with you? If your deddy comes down, he will be in a rage! Go and change into a sari.'

This really couldn't be happening! At this point I tried to retaliate:

'I never wear saris, I don't even know how to put one on and I'm not going to be forced to bloody wear one!'

'First of all don't use that filthy language with me and secondly there is a first time for everything.'

I heard my dad go into the bathroom. Tears started streaming down my mum's face. I knew she would get into shit for this, so I decided to do it for her. Not wear a sari, but instead put on a *shalwar kameez* thingy. I attempted to demonstrate the skill of negotiation. (I'm sure it would have been easier negotiating with a terrorist to release his hostage, because my mum was having none of it.) I was reminding her of the time I wore an Indian suit at my cousin's wedding and how nobody said anything then. She jogged my memory by saying that the fact that I was only twelve years old at the time might have had something to do with it. Oh well. It was worth a try. My head was about to explode. I just wanted to get this over and done with. So I went upstairs to wrap myself in a three-metre length of silk material. I didn't know what the hell I was doing, so sat and waited for my mum to come to the rescue.

Round and round and round I turned, became dizzy in the process and nearly fell over again. My head didn't appreciate it and neither did my mum, who was stressing about being late. Once the safety pins had been put in their places the sari felt a little more secure and less like it was going to fall off. However, I still felt uncomfortable and embarrassed. This wasn't me. I have nothing against the Indian traditional dress, in fact I think it makes all women look stunningly beautiful and very feminine - yep, even you ugly women. I would be happy to wear it at an appropriate event, but I was pissed off that my parents were making me wear one to go and meet a bloke. It was very contradictory when the advice they gave me was to 'be myself'. If I really were to be 'myself', I'm sure they would disown me!

While I was waiting downstairs in the living room, I was pondering about why the sari material is so long and came up with the conclusion that it must have something to do with size equality. The sari gives a false illusion of your body size. Women who are on the chubby side can only wrap the material around their body a limited number of times, whereas skinny women have to wrap it round so many times that they end up looking the same size as the fat ones. Where is the fairness in that?

I hated my parents for making me do this. Everything had happened so quickly that I didn't even have the opportunity to ask my friends what sort of things they spoke about when they had to go through all this and whether it was really as bad as I thought it would be.

Finally we were ready to go. My mum had noticed the carpet burn on my head. Before she had the chance to ask, I sat in the back seat of the car. I was trying to think of a plausible excuse, but my nerves got the better of me. With any luck, I thought, this will not take too long and I can make plans for the rest of the day. Maybe meet up with the girls and tell them about all the happenings in my life or possibly go and see Kieran.

On the way, my dad decided to give his fatherly tips to his little daughter. My mother also had the itch to contribute to some of the advice that he was dishing out. I was too busy texting Ally and giving her the latest update. (Me…wearing a sari!) That was until I heard, 'Don't be too fussy or you will never find anyone.'

I was outraged by that comment. In fact I was ready to have a miniature outburst. They had the audacity to say, 'We are doing this for your future and wellbeing.'

In fact they were doing the very opposite, they were torturing me and driving me insane.

AAAAAARRRRRGGGGGGGGGHHHHHHH!!!!!!!!!!!!!!!!

I didn't say a word. Just stared out of the window wishing that I was in a different country, living my own life the way I wanted to. Less of the fantasy and back to the reality. I was in London, doing nothing. Ahem… I meant looking for a job, living with my controlling parents and almost turning into a hermit!

We turned into a driveway. I should have put the 'I'm not worthy' sign on our banger of a car, for it was parked in the driveway next to three very sexy motors. My jaw nearly hit the floor and I started to dribble. Wow! This place was no humble abode. It was fit for a king and queen. Overwhelmed by their cars and the view of the house from the outside, Miss Nosy-Parker was eager to see what the interior was like. Perhaps this wasn't such a bad idea after all. At the end of the day, if he was a minger then there was always scope for plastic surgery. If it was his personality that was the problem then regrettably even money wouldn't do the trick. The poor soul would have to live with that for the rest of his life! Still I was intrigued.

When I opened the car door and got out, it was so cold that my feet went numb, changing from a light brown colour to a pale blue, all because I had to wear stupid flip-flops. I followed my parents into the house. The door opened before we even got to it; like most Indians, the family must have been peeping through the window, waiting for our arrival. The man smiled and started talking to my dad at the front door. I'm not sure if he had just forgotten to invite us in or whether he wanted us to freeze a little more so we would appreciate the warmth when we did get inside. Meanwhile, my mum and I were standing behind the men, like freezing plums!

Finally we went into the living room. I didn't know where to look. There was a bloke already sitting there flicking the pages of a newspaper. He had the decency to sort of nod, so I nodded in return. I was assuming that was 'him'.

Both sets of parents were chattering away, while I was sitting there like a lemon, feeling self-conscious and inadequate, hoping that they would get their act together by suggesting that we 'go and have our little chat'. I couldn't help but ogle. Actually he was very attractive, so that was a good start. He sat there fixated on the newspaper. It was a little unusual that he seemed not at all bothered about the whole situation. Maybe he was embarrassed by it all as well. He was wearing a black-ribbed Ralph Lauren polo neck with a pair of dark denim jeans. See! His parents didn't make him wear a bloody suit, did they? So far so good, because in my books he had passed the attractive–ugly test with flying colours; now the difficult bit, the personality test.

All of a sudden there was an uncomfortable silence. I thought to myself, if we have to sit here any longer, I'm going to walk out. Just as I finished thinking that, the lady/auntie/his mum/possibly my future mother-in-law, raised her voice. 'Jeevan!' she called. Maybe she didn't realise that he was already sitting in the room, right beside her. So that's what his name was – Jeevan. Why wasn't he paying attention? Was he deaf? I couldn't blame him for that, but why weren't they getting a move on? I gave my dad the evil eye. Again at the top of her voice our hostess shouted, *Jeevan!* Something was definitely wrong here; she was not even looking at him – and why would she be shouting if he was deaf? Lip reading is a tranquil process. I had obviously come to the wrong conclusion.

I turned to look at the living-room door and – uh oh! A tall, weedy male wearing a bottle-green suit, a white shirt and brown shoes stood leaning near the doorframe. His glasses were circular (similar to the ones Harry Potter wears) and they were far too big for his face. The gold-rimmed frames appeared to attract all the attention and he definitely needed a haircut. The curtain hairstyle, greased down, was surely not helping the spots on his forehead disappear and I felt bad thinking it, but at a first glance my initial reaction was, 'Yuk!' So for the past half an hour I had been admiring his bloody brother. No wonder he didn't seem interested or bothered and why the hell was he sitting there in the first place?

I had no option but to go upstairs and talk to Jeevan. Even if I had worn my Spice Girls platform shoes, I probably would have only just managed to level with his shoulder. The younger one had obtained the best features from both parents whereas the older one was less fortunate. I sat on his bed and he sat on a chair. This was so humiliating and I vowed there and then that I was never going to do it again. We introduced ourselves. He was eager to talk about his family, and I was keen to hear about his brother. We spoke about the boring things – education, hobbies and jobs. Even though I was still in a state of shock about the brown shoes and green suit, I dominated the conversation because he had barely anything to say. I couldn't understand why his parents had decided to call him Jeevan (life) because he certainly didn't have one!

Poor Jeevan must have thought that I was a cold, abrupt bitch, and to be honest I didn't need to make much of an effort to achieve that effect. Thank God it was working! After a brief twenty-minute chat he suggested that we should meet again. Perhaps he was a member of one of those masochistic, perverse cults who like impolite, rude and offensive women. I was adamant that we should not meet again. We, or more likely, I, ended our discussion on the basis that it would not work out because we led immensely different lives.

When he asked me again whether I was sure that we were not going to have a second meeting, without another thought, I said that it would never work. Now, my next problem was to try and persuade him to tell his parents that he didn't like me. If I were to say to mine that he wasn't the right guy for me, then all hell would break loose. They would say that I was far too fussy and would give me a lecture on the elementary factor of 'give and take' in relationships.

Most parents are unsympathetic when Indian girls reject boys for their physical appearance or personality. I am often informed by my mother and other married women that after marriage the man can be moulded to the way you want him to be, that they are just like plasticine. I have a different view. Anyway, who these days wants a puppet as their man? Not me, thanks. So I figured that if I told Jeevan to say that he didn't like me, then my parents would have nothing to complain about because technically it would not be my fault. It was so much easier for boys to reject girls than vice versa. So I tried my luck.

I thought he would have been fine with my justified request, but he turned out to be even more of a sucker than I originally thought. The nerd's body language fitted his weedy personality because he said that his willingness to give it a try meant that he couldn't lie by saying that he was not interested. 'Anyway, it's just as difficult for boys to say that they are not interested,' he said in a shaky voice. This was all a front. I knew exactly what the reason was. He wasn't man enough to confront his forceful mother who clearly wore the pants in the family. I had nothing more to say and the matter was left unresolved. I knew what I was going to tell my parents and surprise, surprise, it was not going to be the truth.

Things were going quite well until Jeevan dropped that bombshell on me. After that, we made our way back down the spiral staircase to the living room. Even though I was holding the sari together so I didn't trip up, some of the material was still trailing along behind me.

Conversation ground to a halt as soon as we went back into the living room. Both sets of parents were sporting the infamous Cheshire cat grin. It was sickening! Just as I sat down, a hot cup of Indian chai was handed to me. I hate Indian tea, it's so disgustingly milky and sweet. Whenever we go to a relative's house, I always take the safe option by asking for something cold. In this case I had no choice. Someone had already made that decision for me while I had been upstairs, bored out of my brains. I felt obliged to drink the damn thing, even though my stomach was not feeling at its best. That one cup of tea probably had about seven spoons of sugar in it. I can understand how there might be a causal link between the Asian population and diabetes. Anyway, after a few sips, I held the cup in my hand and was seriously struggling to drink the rest of it.

Yep... they were still nattering away and I was getting very frustrated. I left the teacup on the table and went in search of the bathroom. The bathroom walls had been hand painted with beautiful fine Indian art, so astounding that surely some people would forget what they originally came to do. Although mesmerised by the exquisiteness of the four walls, I was trying to figure out what would be the easiest way to take a pee. Did I hold the sari up or did I pull it down? After grasping some of the fabric in my hands and supporting the rest of it with my arms, I discovered that my mother had pinned the front pleats of my sari to my knickers! Dilemma: Should I detach the safety pin, in which case I'd have trouble putting the sari back together, or could I hold it in for a little longer? I had no choice but to comply with the latter option.

I was inwardly cursing my mother. I stood by the living-room door, hoping that this would be a subtle hint for us to get going. Deep in conversation, the others didn't even notice me. I was patiently waiting for a pause in the conversation so I could suggest that we go home, but these people had so much to say that they didn't even take a breath! So I had to interrupt. After all, I did have other responsibilities, such as not wetting myself! A few minutes later, they all stood up and made their way to the main entrance door where another conversation started. Before it got any further, I quickly added my 'bye, adios, au revoir, toodaloo, ciao, sayonara' and off we went.

Heading back home, I received the Spanish Inquisition as soon as I informed my parents that nothing would go further with Jeevan. Why, why, why? They kept questioning every word that came out of my mouth. When they tried to make me feel guilty, I said that he was not interested in me, and that automatically shut them up No one said a word for the rest of the journey. They were pissed off that it didn't work out and I was upset and felt that they wanted to get rid of me. No matter what the consequences, I was not going to settle down with someone just for the sake of doing so or to keep my parents happy.

As soon as we arrived back home, I dashed upstairs and went to empty my bladder, then got back into bed to catch up on sleep that had been disturbed and interrupted by the toxic liquids from the previous evening.

6
Knock Knock - Who's There?

A few hours later, I felt as though I had been dead to the world for absolutely ages. Nevertheless I still needed more sleep to fully rejuvenate myself. I could have easily done so, had I not heard the doorbell ring. We were not expecting anyone, so who could it be? Unexpectedly (and uninvited) a family friend - my dad's aunt's daughter-in-law's son - came with his whiny wife and their three toffee-nosed children, all of whom rudely walked into the living room and made themselves comfortable on our settee. He was a friend of my dad's younger brother too.

If I had opened the door, I would have sent them on their way before they even had the chance to ask if my parents were home. Unfortunately, my mother was far too polite to send anyone away. In fact, she would even stand at the door listening to Jehovah's Witnesses whilst they tried to talk her into becoming a Christian, or sales people who sometimes forget to breathe because they have so much to say, trying to sell their useless commodities. They wouldn't give her a chance to say that she was not in the least bit interested in their spiel but I, on the other hand, never offer them the opportunity to inaugurate. Within a minute of opening the door, I take great pleasure in closing it again - that is, just before they open their gob to free the words that are about to come out of it. I wished we could do the same with the family that had come to visit.

Uncle Rajesh Parek aka Mr Vain was totally in denial of his age. He had been thirty-five for at least ten years or so. In everyone's eyes he could do no better. He had the perfect job, perfect house, perfect family and a perfect lifestyle. However, I had a feeling that there were plenty of skeletons in his closet, and that he was cleverly hiding them all. The wife, Auntie Mira Parek, was ten years younger than Uncle Rajesh. She was extremely boastful and had a lavish lifestyle, doing nothing in short measures. My aunt was a big spender. Despite her weekly facials at Harvey Nichols, she still looked ten years older than Uncle Raj's real age! Her husband was the extreme opposite and accounted for every single penny that he spent. He was commonly known as 'Stingy Scrooge'. The little rugrats (more like rugbrats) had taken after their mother. They were spoiled and a pain in the arse. Uncle Raj worked as a medical consultant at The Woodside Manor Hospital, where he spent most of his time supposedly working.

'Oh hello, Naina.'

'Actually, it's Nina,' (you useless tosser). 'Hi Uncle, how are you?'

'Nina, Naina - what's the difference?' he replied.

I gave him a dirty look and chose not to stoop to his level. Then I sat down, ready to answer the same old questions they always asked me.

'So what are you doing now? A levels, is it?'

'Er, you asked me that question last year and I told you I had already graduated.' (How stupid do you feel now?) 'Don't worry, Uncle, the ageing process has a negative effect on the memory.' He didn't take that comment too well.

'Well, at least you're not scrounging off the government. Where are you working then?' he said smugly.

I was just about to make him feel like he had put his foot in it yet again, but my mother quickly interrupted and answered for me. 'Oh, she is getting money from the government because she is working with the Civil Service, aren't you, *beta*?'

Why couldn't I just say that I was claiming government benefits? It wasn't my fault that I couldn't find a job. Now I had to lie about something I knew nothing about to none other than a consultant.

I was saved by the bell, thanks to two of the rugbrats who started to fidget and were already getting tired of each other's company. Auntie Mira didn't take the opportunity to sit down, so they must have come for a reason. The third little one was sitting on the settee with his elbows on his knees and his hands covering his cheeks, looking extremely miserable and bored. I was hoping that they wouldn't stay long enough for us to have to offer them tea. Luck was on my side.

The uppity Auntie Mira opened her purse and took out an invitation for a dinner party they were having for their crystal anniversary. Personally, I think that she didn't want to invite us, but Uncle Rajesh must have insisted thinking that it would look bad if they didn't. They said they had to go and deliver the invitations to other houses, and set off. God knows why they didn't just post them. Tight-arses.

Great...now we felt obliged to go and attend this stupid dinner party. Auntie Mira said her goodbyes and waited for her other half to follow her out.

'Oh, and I've invited your brother too,' she told Dad, 'so it should be a good reunion.'

Oh great, I hate them. Well not the parents, just their kids.

I sat in front of the TV, staring at a blank screen because it was on standby and the remote control was not at arm's reach. I felt so lethargic that I couldn't be bothered to move and find it. I then fell into deep thought, wondering why my life had taken a turn for the worse. Perhaps it had always been that way, but all these years I had just been oblivious to it. By now I was convinced that I was suffering from uni-polar depression, or some other sort of emotional disorder.

I had nothing planned for the week ahead so I went to investigate further the location and time of that stupid party and to see if it was an absolute necessity for me to attend. It's not the fact that I don't enjoy events like that - especially if there is food involved and I'm not cooking it - but it is more the people that I will be encountering. Everyone seems to have serious underlying issues with each other, but on the surface they are very nice to each other. My three first cousins illustrate my point extremely well.

The daughters of Uncle Amir (Dad's brother) and Auntie Seema are called Tina, Rakhi and Asha. (I call them Anastacia, Drizzilla and Drinastacia, after the ugly sisters in *Cinderella*.) The first has an attitude problem, the second is an airhead bimbo and the third is a mixture of both. I try to avoid them at all costs, because I have come to the conclusion that they are *evil*. I guarantee that they could play the star role in any of the Stephen King movies and they wouldn't even have to act! Thankfully we only tend to bump into them at weddings and other Asian cultural events. Unfortunately, they were going to be at this dinner party. Strangely Ana, Driz and Drin's parents are as sweet as pie, and they absolutely adore my sister and me. God knows how they produced such vindictive children. I can understand there being one troubled child in the family, but all three? That's a bit extreme.

Ana is a receptionist at a car showroom. At the age of twenty-five she has nothing to show for herself but a long list of men with whom she has slept, half of whom are probably married. At least I suppose she spreads her favours fairly, as they come from all walks of life.

Driz is the complete opposite. In her case 'the lights are on but no one's at home'. She is twenty-three and has worked as a telesales administrator since the age of sixteen. There are no promotion prospects - due, I dare say - to lack of brainpower. There is not much to say about Driz except that her actions speak louder than her words.

Drin is 'sour sixteen'. Following in her sisters' footsteps, she has also become a common foe. However, she has a beautiful physique, being tall, slim and very attractive, with long dark brown hair and fair skin that is annoyingly blemish-free. Unfortunately, she lacks the personality to match. This was a relief in a way - otherwise she'd have had it all. Everyone is puzzled as to why she never took up modelling, but no one has ever dared to ask in case they get their head bitten off. It was Drin's responsibility to find out all the gossip and report back to the Ugly and Dumb Sisters. There's something else about the Horrible Three: they come from east London. Now there's nothing wrong with that, so don't get all hoity-toity, you Brick Laners, but my cousins are the perfect example of the stereotypical Cockney with a splash of Bollywood mixed in.

This is only a taster; unfortunately I have plenty more cousins who are not all that nice either. But, none of them are anywhere near as nasty as these three girls. They invent malicious rumours, then spread them - which leads to terrible confrontations affecting family politics and often results in war. This is why I try to avoid occasions where I have to associate with dangerous people and show civility towards them.

It's just not me!

7
Preparations

9 am the day prior to the party. The phone rings. Mother answers it.

'Hello'

'Hello, it's Mira. *Kesay ho?*'

I was sitting next to Mum and could hear every word. Auntie Mira has a voice like a goddamn foghorn.

'Oh, I'm fine…you sound a bit panicked, is something the matter?'

'I am having a panic attack. I really don't think I will finish cooking all the different types of food in time…what shall I do? I phoned up the catering people but now they are booked up for another event.'

Mum frowned. It wasn't in her nature to turn down a plea for help.

'Well, you know I would come to help but today I have volunteered to look after Jim's little one. He's our next-door neighbour.'

'I know you are busy. The reason I called was to see if Nina would be kind enough to come and help me? She can stay the night. I would be forever grateful.'

'I'm sure she would *love* to come and help you,' my mother

said, ignoring my gasp of horror. That way she can learn a bit of cooking too. As soon as she is ready, I will send her round.'

'Okay, bye – and see you tomorrow!'

'Bye.'

Trust Auntie Mira to call at this time in the morning. Honestly, even though I had not committed a crime (yet), I felt like I was serving a permanent sentence of community service.

Still, at least it wasn't my gran phoning to get me to help her with the household chores. I hate going to her house. It always smells funny, as if it has not been aired for a couple of thousand years. There is enough dust to construct a mountain and the wooden floor is always coated with sticky stuff, usually consisting of juice spillage that has not been wiped up for a few days. The worst thing is that she walks around the house using her Zimmer frame, wearing no house slippers so that her socks leave bits of fluff when she walks over the spillage. Nevertheless, she is a lovely old lady who never asks for help even when it is badly needed. I made a resolution there and then to go and see her when this stupid 'crystal anniversary' party was over, and give her place a good 'bottoming' as they say oop North.

Grandpa is the complete opposite; he is a moany ol' git who thinks that the world should revolve around him. A little cough and he reckons he's dying. Everyone must stop whatever they are doing and run around at his beck and call. They are both extremely wealthy, but live like paupers. My grandpa believes that money should be kept for rainy days. He has definitely lost the plot, since they have enough dosh to last them through another reincarnation. Although they both want to go back to India, Grandpa is a shrewd old man, and is reluctant to lose out on the few pounds that the UK government gives to pensioners. He would rather suffer the cold and being trapped indoors for half the year. Gradually, one by one, we have given up on those two. Every time I go round to their house, Grandma has trouble recognising me, and I have to repeat my name three times before she even gets that right. Grandpa never fails to remind me that if I lived in India, he would have married me off at the age of sixteen! Somehow I tolerate it and have learned to ignore him.

Out of sympathy, I recently went and helped Gran clean the entire place. Ever since then, she gets confused and sees me, not as her granddaughter, but as her cleaner. This is the kind of thing you run into when you're a good little Indian girl.

'The poor thing was so stressed over this party,' my mother twittered. 'See, Nina, you might as well stay the night and help her tomorrow as well. It will be good practice for you. When you get married, you will have dinner parties too.'

Grrr. 'But Mum – you know I don't even *like* the woman! She probably called up everyone else first, and after being rejected, used us as a last resort.'

'Don't speak of your Auntie in that way, she is a nice woman.' My mother was annoyed. She just can't face the truth, that's her problem. 'Stop giving everybody a hard time, Nina. This will give you a good opportunity to get to know her.'

I didn't want to get to know her. 'I will feel ill at ease,' I sulked.

'Don't use big words that I don't understand.' Actually, as a point of reference, they are three little words. 'Why can't you be more like your sister?'

It was like we were playing tennis with words. I kept throwing at her the reasons for not going, and she kept returning the reasons for helping Auntie Mira. I knew exactly why she wanted me to go. Uncle Rajesh was very well known and respected in our community, so if it was acknowledged that we socialised in the same circle (with the elite), then my mother thought there might be more potential marriage proposals from suitable boys. Although I was bitterly annoyed, I ended up giving in to her. After all, I supposed I might end up having a better time at her house than at home. (I think I was in denial again.)

Hold on a minute! Auntie Mira needed help with the cooking. So I would be of no use anyway; in fact, I might just make things worse and get in the way. I had an idea! I would phone Auntie Mira and simply tell her that I had other plans (which were to sit and read in the back garden, while soaking up the few rays of sun) and that my mum had not realised this was the case. Piece of cake! The moment Mum popped out, I lifted the receiver and dialled 14713.

When Auntie Mira answered, she could not stop thanking me for promising to come round. I interrupted and informed her of the bad news, at which point there was a pin-drop silence. I thought she might have fainted! Her voice sounded shaky and I didn't know what to do. My initial reaction was to tell her that I was joking and that is exactly what I managed to do.

What a total mug! Since when did I start to develop a guilty conscience? I could not believe that I had wormed my way out of this mess only to land myself back up to my neck in it. I thought it was best to carry out my good deed for the day and avoid the remorse that would have been outstanding had I not fulfilled my duty.

I dashed over to Ally's house, before making my way to Auntie Mira's. Ally was still in her pyjamas, hair everywhere, and was lying in her bed filling out a competition entry form from *Fashion* magazine. The prize was a choice between a two-week trip to a health farm in Thailand or attending a prestigious movie award ceremony in India's capital, New Delhi. I told her that she would never win, and although she agreed, she said she felt lucky and was going to send the entry form in anyway.

The lazy tart insisted that she had been intending to make an appearance at my house, but evidently I beat her to it. She had her own issues with her parents: they were on her back about 'doing the Asian thing' and getting married, having kids and looking after her husband. What they didn't know was that she had been seeing someone for nearly three years and was planning to get married to him.

Ally met Dylan at University. They made the perfect couple, for he loved her just as much as she loved him. However, there was a slight hitch. He was not Indian – in fact he was not even Asian. Although fascinated by Indian culture, he was actually Australian. After graduation, he walked straight into a job as a financial consultant in one of the most prestigious banks in Central London. A couple of months after Ally started dating him, Dylan and I became really close friends.

Difficulties arose when they had their arguments, because I was stuck in the middle. I sometimes envied their relationship. Dylan is good-looking and has a great personality. So I still have faith that attractive blokes with a personality do exist in this world...I just have to keep looking and be patient!

The problem Ally faces now is that her time spent with Dylan has been reduced dramatically because she is back living with her parents. In order to see him, she has to sneak out and I have to cover for her.

There was a time not so long ago, around Valentine's Day, when I got myself into a bit of a pickle. Ally was doing the dirty and had told her parents that she was staying at my house, when in fact she was looking forward to her long-awaited rendezvous with Dylan at his place. When her mum called up unexpectedly, asking to speak to her, straight away the word 'loo' popped into my mind, which was rather foolish because that just prolonged the phone call and I had to tell her that Ally would return her call. Ten minutes later, her mother called again. I was petrified and desperately trying to think of another excuse. I am never short of ideas, and yes, this sounds a tad far-fetched, I know, but I was willing to give it a try...I answered the phone in the usual manner and then in a muffled voice pretended to be Ally.

Luckily, it was nothing serious. It turned out that Ally had to be home early the next day because they had to attend a distant relative's marriage ceremony at a register office. That whole night, I tried to save both our arses by phoning Ally's mobile, only to find that it was permanently switched off. It was ironic how Ally and I were both having a sleepless night. It was her fault, yet she was having lots of 'under the duvet' action whilst I was overloaded with worries about never, ever seeing the light of day again.

I won't forget that night in a hurry. I set my alarm clock for some ridiculous hour in the morning, so I could try calling Ally. Thank God she had had the decency to switch her phone back on.

In her state of panic, instead of going straight home she bombed it back to mine. I was ready to give her a piece of my mind, but it wasn't the time or the place. Hastily I dug out an Indian suit and helped her put it on. We sprayed her all over with 'Jean Paul Gaultier' and I lent her my favourite earrings. By the time we had finished, she didn't look too bad. Goodbye, slapper. Hello, good little Indian girl. Then she phoned for a cab and set off. God! One day Alisha Desai will be the death of me.

After all that kerfuffle, it was somewhat of an anti-climax when another guest at the ceremony snootily informed her that she was wearing the skirt inside out. She felt like a right moron. The highlight of the day was that there was nowhere to change – so in all the photos she wears a beautiful smile and an inside-out skirt. She could start off a new fashion trend. Then again, maybe not.

As usual we had plenty to talk about but not enough time. This was only a pit stop. I had to rush off if I was to get to Auntie Mira's house before dark. I have already described my troublesome experiences with public transport, and now it was time to face those dreadful buses and tube trains again.

51

Carrying a small bag containing my overnight things and party clothes, I decided to take a stroll through the park, thus combing a bit of fresh air with a short cut to the Underground station. The weather in the month of May is always unpredictable. One day it's pouring down with rain and then the next day is baking hot. Thankfully the sun was shining brightly and my black T-shirt was absorbing every tiny ray. Primary schoolchildren were playing 'rounders' and 'quick cricket' and I wondered where they found the energy to run about in this scorching weather.

As I walked past, watching the mothers and nannies playing with their babies, a tennis ball suddenly whacked me in the chest. Someone had thrown the damn thing with so much force that I honestly thought they were out to kill me. If it had hit me on the head, they might well have succeeded! I had a quick peek down the neck of my T-shirt just to make sure that there was no immediate swelling. (I didn't want to be the 'three-boob woman'!) All clear – there was no dent, no swelling and no bruising. Assuming that the ball had been thrown by one of the school players, I picked it up to lob it back at them.

Within a matter of seconds a tremendously vicious-looking dog was heading straight for me. I was going to suggest to the owner that she should consider sending her pet to compete in the dog-track races, but first things first: I had a duty to protect myself. The tennis ball was still in my hands, my trembling legs felt like lead and I was frozen like a statue...if I waited any longer I was going to be defrosted meat! The dog was salivating heavily and looked as though he had missed out on yesterday's breakfast, lunch and dinner!

I had no time to think. I was so fearful, I headed toward some bushes, not even sure what I was going to do when I got there. The next thing I knew, the bloody dog was right behind me and I could hear the female owner shouting his name in the background. The dog got hold of one trouser leg and started pulling it. I began to scream and hit him with my plastic bag, and then I threw the tennis ball at his face. The ball bounced off and the dog erratically followed it. If only I had let go of the ball in the first place, none of this would have happened. I was shaken up but managed to put on a brave face.

'I'm gonna git the NSPCA on to ya,' the woman said in a high-pitched voice. She was wearing torn, ragged clothes (probably the dog's fault!) and with a nose for fragrances, I had no trouble identifying hers. Today she was wearing the 'BO de toilette'. Ms Big Silver Hoops and Crooked Stained Teeth had the sheer insolence to complain about how I had treated her wretched animal.

'No! Actually it's the RSPCA and *I* am going to contact *them*. Your dog is a hazardous creature when out in public places. Look what it's done to me.' I was too scared to say any more.

'Shaat it, before I tell 'im to finish you off!' she shouted confidently as she walked away. I got up and brushed the excess grass off my clothes. A lady passing by asked if she could help. My left trouser leg looked like it had taken a trip down the shredding machine, but fortunately I had no scratches, although I thought I might have to treat myself to one of those 'backside' tetanus injections to make sure that I had not been contaminated with some vile disease from the dog's slavering jaws.

I thought this type of 'dog-chasing stuff' only happened in cartoons. Now every time I walk through a park (which will be hardly ever - especially on my own) I will have to be aware not only of perverts and weirdoes, but dogs as well. What is this country coming to?

As I carried on walking to the station with my ripped trouser leg, I felt embarrassed and mentally prepared myself for the discomfiting stares that people were bound to give me. However, no one batted an eyelid. The best thing about living in London is that people don't care. They are far too busy to be bothered by badly-mauled young women.

At the station I went into the public toilets and changed into my party trousers. By now I had realised it was going to be one of those days when shit happens, non-stop. Maybe it was a sign that I was not meant to be out and about or even to go to Auntie Mira's house. The train was delayed – when isn't it? – so I bought some trashy magazines to read with loads of celebrity gossip inside. Finally I reached Harrow station where Auntie Mira was waiting patiently in her car. I still felt far too traumatised to tell her what had happened earlier and as a result, the silence was a little awkward in the car.

Uncle Rajesh's house was situated in a secluded residential area on the outskirts of Harrow. There had been lots of refurbishment since the last time we had visited the three-storey house *en famille*.

An indoor, heated swimming pool had been installed on the top floor. Uncle Raj, yet again, was counting all the pennies and believed that in the long run it would be cheaper to have a pool than pay an extortionate membership fee for his three children to have swimming lessons at a private gym. I wouldn't be surprised if he charged the little rugbrats' friends a fee for coming to swim in his pool during the summer holidays. A fitness freak, Uncle Raj had converted half of the top floor into a state-of-the-art gym and the other part into a kids' play area. The rest of the house was elegant and modern with no clutter and plenty of space.

The private development where his house stood consisted of eight detached houses; from the outside they looked quite small, but inside they were spacious. Once again Auntie Mira thanked me and informed me that she appreciated what I was doing for her.

As far as I was concerned, simply getting here had nearly finished me off, and now there were all those damn preparations to start on. The day's work was only just beginning.

8
The Parek Residence

As I entered, I noticed that the house was pleasantly scented with a spring fragrance. I was shown to the downstairs guestroom to wash my hands. I could instantly tell that Uncle Raj had no say in the interior furnishings because most of them came from exclusive 'home furniture stores' or home exhibitions. None were from B&Q or MFI (Made For Indians). Not that there's anything wrong with that - I'm no snob - but Auntie Mira hated the fact that most Indians copy each other and have exactly the same things in their houses.

As I walked into the living room to take a quick look, a beautiful oil painting of the family stared right back at me. The walls were elegant and plain, and the leather sofas were unencumbered by 'throws'. I never did understand why so many Indian houses that I visited had settees covered with fabric, which happened to be a completely different colour from the sofa. What was the point of that? Similarly, they sometimes had bubblewrap-style plastic carpet protector on top of the carpet in the hallway to prevent it from getting dirty when people walked over it. I personally don't see how a carpet can get dirty if visitors take off their shoes before entering the house. People's socks can't be as dirty as the soles of their shoes, can they? If it really is beneficial and doesn't look tacky, then why don't you see this bubblewrap shit in *non*-Asian households? It must be – yes, you've guessed it – an Asian thing.

My eyes nearly popped out of their sockets when I saw the big, phat plasma-screen TV on the wall. With the lights dimmed, a handful of popcorn and a mini-sized tub - actually let's go for the pint-sized tub - of Häagen Dazs, it could easily be mistaken for a cinema. I was eager to see the rest of the house, but promised to give myself the grand tour when the kids got home; that way I could use them as a legitimate excuse.

I went into the kitchen. Auntie Mira had changed into a pair of joggers and advised me to wear something old, because we were about to do 'a hell of a lot of cooking'. It was a deciding factor between wearing my 'dog bitten' trousers or my pyjamas! She then started to laugh (I had a feeling it was at my expense). I was right, for she suggested that I put my trousers in the freezer for a while. Of course, my natural reaction was to ask why. After she had stopped chuckling, she informed me that I had white chewing gum stuck to my behind.

While she wiped her tears of laughter, I was about to release tears of bitterness because some idiot, who had never heard of a dustbin, had yet again exposed me to ridicule. Why can't we be civilised about this? Banning the damn stuff would keep Britain a tidier place. There would be no kids blowing Hubba Bubba bubbles that then explode in their face and make a mess, there would be no disgusting chewing gum underneath school tables and obviously there would be none on my f★★★★g trousers!! The ban works in Singapore, so why wouldn't it work here? When I govern the country, this will be one of my first pieces of legislation.

Well, at least it broke the ice. I explained that I had had a little accident and torn my other pair on my way to the station. She immediately said that I was welcome to borrow a pair of her old joggers. She was about ten feet taller than me – well, most people are – and at least two sizes bigger. Even though they were elasticated at the waist, I had to wear the joggers in true Simon Cowell style, really high up under my boobs. Irritatingly, I still had to keep hoisting them up every five minutes when they slid down and started to show the stringy bit of my thong.

Maybe I had been too hasty in my judgements of Auntie Mira. She didn't seem that bad after all. Call it intuition, but I had a feeling that she was quite decent underneath it all but felt unappreciated and misunderstood. However, I also knew this was going to be a disastrous day. It had started off badly enough and my attitude was that it could only get worse.

Before we actually started preparing the food, we sat down to have a coffee. Having showed her my new 'dog designer' trousers, I started to tell Auntie Mira about my little ordeal. Although she tried to show some sympathy, she could not help but laugh again and, looking at it retrospectively, neither could I. Auntie Mira no longer wanted me to put 'Auntie' in front of her name. She said that it made her feel ancient. It also instantly opened up the gates for a new friendship.

By doing a bit of subtle detective work, I soon found out that Uncle Raj and Mira were having problems with their marriage. Whilst he was gallivanting around the city, she was left at home looking after the children and doing the housework. She had no one to confide in. Before the conversation became too deep and meaningful, I thought I would cheer her up with another one of my comical stories, despite the fact that it meant I would be the butt of the joke. She chuckled at it, then told me a few things about herself and her background.

Mira was born in East Africa and came to England when she was in her early twenties. I was unaware that she had had aspirations to become a lawyer just before her parents married her off. Uncle Raj did not let her finish her studies and expected her to stay at home and look after the children because he wanted to be the sole breadwinner. That's probably why she came across as being so restless and discontented.

After that, I saw her in a totally different light. I no longer thought that she was an indolent cow who lacked common sense and just wanted to sit on her arse and do nothing all day. She felt deflated and unmotivated, that was all. It is funny how things can appear so very different on the surface from what they really are deep down.

There were numerous recipe books out on the table, and I had a bad feeling that I was not the only one who knew nothing about cooking. We chopped up billions of vegetables and stir-fried them. Making the pastry was the challenging bit so I decided to leave that to Mira while I put myself in charge of adding the various Indian spices to the vegetables. Soon there was flour strewn across the floor and vegetable peelings covered the work surfaces.

I lost track of all the things Mira was doing at any one time. They say that we females are good at multi-tasking, but this was taking the mick. By two o' clock, we had practically finished preparing everything for the next day's bash. I don't think I had been much help really; all I did was keep an eye on the food that was cooking on the stove and from time to time stir it. So there really wasn't much point having me there in the first instance. It took longer to clean up the kitchen than it did cooking in it! Apart from the earlier mishaps, I pretty much had an enjoyable day with Mira.

After we had left the kitchen looking immaculate once more, we went off to have a well-deserved soak in their Jacuzzi. I had deliberately brought my swimming cossie for this purpose. I was going to be a typical Indian and make the most of my day and night at this place. I could not understand how Mira had such a healthy appetite but at the same time be so slim. I would never have thought that she was a mother of three. Either she had a high metabolism or was just a 'worry guts' who didn't put on weight.

The conversation drifted from what I got up to in my university life (I had to lie of course) to my love-life (I had to lie again!) to her married life. She showed no affection when speaking of Uncle Raj and I sensed that even this crystal anniversary was a shambles, maybe not for him but undeniably for her. I felt sympathy for her plight: I would never be able to live her life, that of a bird trapped in a gilded cage. She told me she worried about her husband being unfaithful, but I scrapped that idea before she became paranoid about it. Uncle Raj would never even have the thought run through his head, I reassured her.

Speaking of the devil, Uncle Raj chose that moment to phone and say that he was running late, and suggested that we have dinner without him. We had both done a year's worth of cooking in a couple of hours and had still more to look forward to the next day. Neither of us could bear the thought of going back into the kitchen to get a glass of water, let alone cook a meal! So we decided to order a Chinese takeaway and spend the evening watching a movie. The children were staying at their grandparents' house so whilst Mira went to rent a movie and pick up the takeaway, I gave myself a quick tour of the house.

Just as I expected, the rest of the house was beautiful. However I could not help but feel that it lacked a 'lived-in' atmosphere. Tidy and soulless, that's what it was. The walls were very thin, too; it reminded me of the times at uni, when my housemates and I were convinced that a few thick cardboard dividers joined together would have done a better job. Maybe that was one of the reasons why Uncle Raj and Mira kept the walls bare; if they hammered any nails in, the house might fall down.

I was a little anxious about sleeping downstairs, as the room was adjacent to the kitchen, and the dishwasher and washing machine were both in use and making as much noise as possible. I hoped that the humming, swishing and spinning would have stopped by the time I went to bed. I would just have to wait and see. I changed into my pyjamas, got some plates and cutlery ready, and whilst waiting for Mira, reflected on my peculiar day. I chuckled to myself when I thought about the incident in the park. Thirty years ago, sitting sniggering like this, for no apparent reason, would have been considered a sign of madness. I would have spent the rest of my life in a mental institution with psychos who really were insane in the membrane! In fact, if someone caught me doing that now, I'm sure they would still think I was 'a bit funny in the head'. However, I wouldn't be institutionalised for it.

I had mentioned to Mira that I was in the mood to see a funny movie. It would be nice to laugh at someone else for a change. I was hoping she would come back with something along the lines of *Bridget Jones's Diary* or *My Best Friend's Wedding*. If she decided to bring back a psychological thriller, she was going to watch it on her lonesome. I was already apprehensive about sleeping in the downstairs bedroom, I wasn't going to scare myself even more by watching stuff about a psycho-killer on the loose. At the beginning of the movie, I always console myself by mentally repeating, 'It's not real, it's fiction, they're only acting', but once engrossed in the plot I always end up frightening myself. That is one of the reasons why I don't watch *Crimewatch*. As it goes, I would have serious trouble spotting the Most Wanted Criminal even if he or she tripped over my leg.

I was a little lost in this unfamiliar setting. As I walked around the big sitting room, I looked into the gigantic pot which contained a very large banana tree, expecting to find a secret camera or some other *You've Been Framed*-style gadgets. These are usually kept in places such as behind photo frames or ornaments. But seeing that there were none in sight, I thought the next best place to check would be the banana tree! Not that I was about to do anything stupid, I was just probing.

The home was full of very complex electronic gadgets. I was mystified by the number of remote controls for their TV, for instance. Each one had about a hundred buttons on it. I couldn't believe this; I was intimidated by a bloody remote control! I couldn't even see where the on/off button was. Usually they are situated at the top left- and right-hand corners…but obviously like much of the Pareks' belongings, this was one of a kind.

As I heard the key turn in the lock, I was still trying to work out how to get a picture on the screen. I didn't want to give the impression of being totally thick, because I'm not. Can I be blamed if modern computerised sci-fi style gadgets have a problem communicating with me? So I decided to stop fannying about with that stupid piece of what looked like a silver brick with lots of buttons and instead quickly picked up the local newspaper. I sat down to look at the pictures and read the headlines of the budget stories that somehow made it into the newspaper.

I was ravenous! Although not an ardent fan of Chinese food (it is always my last option for takeaway because I find the dishes greasy and very bland), I was ready to eat everything that was on offer! That included the chopsticks even though I don't use them (tried but just can't do it!) and usually settle for a fork or spoon. When Mira switched the TV on, only then did I realise that I was using the wrong control to begin with! Ready to watch the film, I enquired about the title.

Hmm . . . Not exactly what I was expecting. She had rented out a comedy but it was not in English. It was a bloody Hindi movie. From past experiences these don't actually have to be a comedy, since the whole thing is a joke. It is usually three torturous hours of 'Bollywood wannabe Hollywood' type of material. The superficial storylines and over-dramatic acting remind me more of a pantomime than a movie.

Most Hindi films have the theme of good versus evil. The characters usually include a hero, a villain and a damsel in distress. This is not the problem, it is the fact that most films have exactly the same plot: boy meets girl, boy falls in love with girl, girl is about to be married off to 'the villain', then the boy becomes a hero and rescues the girl. The parents find out the baddie's ulterior motives. In the finale, the hero kills the villain and they all live happily ever after. Needless to say, it would never be classed as a Hindi film without breaking into song and dance routine every ten minutes. Whether or not it fits in with the script is a different matter altogether!

During that one song the acting couple change their costumes about seven times. A few years ago, for the male it was tight jeans or tight black trousers and vest tops and for the female it was changing from one sari to the next. As time progressed, the dance routines became raunchier and the costumes have changed from conservative saris to *shalwar kameez*. More recently, we have seen the introduction of trousers that are practically stuck to the skin and skimpy halter-neck tops; these in turn have been replaced with mini-skirts and boob-tubes. Some outfits are so outrageous, strippers wear more. While all the old mums and grannies complain about the girls being practically naked and how times have changed, the dads and gramps gawk at the screen (with their jaws touching the floor) while trying to look uninterested.

Nowadays the modern films have started to show a few scenes whereby the lovers do actually kiss on screen (don't be stupid, not a full-on snog, more like a slight touch of the lips). However, even that's embarrassing to watch with the elders. Yet many of us would feel a lot more comfortable watching these kinds of movies with our parents and relatives than we would a Hollywood movie. The certificate rating of fifteen or eighteen is bound to have a passionate sex scene that feels like it goes on for an eternity. That's when no one knows where to look and all of a sudden everybody has the urge to visit the toilet all at once. Or the best one is if it's on TV, when one of the parents (usually the mum!) will have the remote control to hand and will switch channels for about three minutes so everyone misses the action. That's what I call family mortification!

Conclusion: Hindi movies are watchable if you are in a slagging-off mood – in which case no one else watching it will appreciate your company and waspish comments. They are also good for a laugh at the choreography and the stereotypical gender roles where the good wife worships the ground her husband walks on and is a 'Delia Smith' in the kitchen. As far as I'm concerned, these movies belong in the 'fantasy' genre. I'm sure the way in which Asian parents think is reinforced by these damn silly movies.

Within half an hour I was already distracted and found myself making rude little comments about the actors in my head. To be honest, I would have preferred to have an early night. But I sat there in silence, staring at the screen, and my eyes started to blink for longer periods of time. I was falling asleep. Mira was in her element. She loved every minute of the film, while I, on the contrary, was trying so hard just to keep awake.

At a quarter past twelve I finally entered my grand suite. I could have fallen asleep on the adorable fluffy carpet but the bed was far more tempting. I was running low on energy but felt an irresistible desire to run from the door and jump on to the bed. I did just that and – oops! I bounced right off, hoping that my arse had not made a dent in the floor. The noise was loud enough for Mira to come racing in to find me flat on my face.

I hadn't realised that the king-sized bed contained lots and lots of water. Great! I had never slept on a waterbed before, and was quite looking forward to a night on the sea! As soon as I got in, though, I was wide awake. Every time I fidgeted I could hear the water slap about. It felt like I was sleeping on a big, fat hot-water bottle. I kept thinking something was going to jump out of the cupboards, but soon enough I fell asleep.

At some ludicrous hour Uncle Raj stumbled into the house completely rat-arsed! I lay in my bed listening to his drunken speech; it was difficult not to because the walls were wafer-thin. Only then did I become aware that he was not talking to himself. A female was also present.

What on earth was she doing here at this time of the night? Her voice was high-pitched and she was giggling. She must have had one too many cocktails too. When I could hear no more talking I began to wonder what they were doing. Surely, Uncle Raj would not be stupid enough to bring his lover home, would he? How could he fondle Miss Floozy under his roof while the wife was fast asleep upstairs? The cheek of the man!

Before it went any further I had to do something... otherwise the walls were going to reveal something I did not particularly wish to hear. Anyway, I wanted to see this woman who was aiding the destruction of my uncle's marriage.

Should I intrude or shouldn't I, was the question. I was trying to think of an excuse to go into the kitchen, and also contemplating whether it would be safe to enter the danger zone. I felt I had to do something about it so in the end I got out of bed and went to fetch a glass of water. I deliberately made more noise than necessary while approaching and entering the kitchen.

Uncle Raj was mortified when he saw me; he didn't know what to do. It was too late to bundle the stupid tart into one of the cupboards. He made an effort to remove his hands which were happily clamped around her bottom. Her back was facing me; all I could see was her mid-length hair that was covered with bleached strands (definitely a home jobby). That was until she turned around...

I couldn't believe my eyes. I think I liked the look of her back better than I did the front, not because she was drop dead gorgeous and I was jealous...Oh no. Uncle Raj's fancy woman was only my cousin Tina - you know, the slapper I mentioned earlier.

I was more embarrassed than she was and didn't know where to look. She mumbled something but I was far too shocked to hear what was being said. The silence in the kitchen was killing me. The atmosphere was filled with animosity, so much so that one could have cut it with a knife.

At moments like these, I always wish that I could turn back time. No one said anything and after a minute or so, Tina picked up her bag and walked straight out of the door. Uncle Raj went after her. They were bickering and although I tried to eavesdrop, I couldn't hear a word they were saying. Eventually, the front door slammed shut and Uncle Raj came back into the kitchen.

'It's not what you think,' he said.

'Oh come on - it's exactly what I think. How long has this been going on?' I said.

'I don't have to answer to you!'

'No, you don't, but I'm sure you'll be extremely happy to answer to everyone at the party, when they find out about this. And if I don't mention it then I'll practise my investigative questioning on my cousin. I'm sure it won't take her too long to confess to exactly what she was doing round here with you in the early hours of the morning.' I added sarcastically.

'Okay look, it was just a one-off. I met her at this bar and things escalated. Nothing would've happened though!'

In a way, I found I was not in the least bit surprised about all these developments; at the back of my mind I had been expecting something of the sort from him...just not in the way that it had actually occurred – at his house, and with my cousin!

'What will it take to keep you silent?'

I felt like a corrupt police officer being offered hush money from a criminal. He said it so comfortably that anyone would have thought he was used to buying his way out of tricky situations.

'At least think about it,' he said as he walked out.

Once back in bed, I pondered over this dilemma I had produced for myself. As if my life was not complicated enough already! It wasn't a situation I wanted to get involved in, but I had no choice. Should I tell Mira or not? I tossed and turned, the waterbed irritated me and I was not looking forward to the next morning.

9
The Dinner Party

The tables had turned. In the early hours of the morning, the suffering of insomnia had transformed into the affliction of narcolepsy. Had I not experienced the phenomenon of the 'falling sensation' - that is, when you feel as though you are falling from a great height and your body suddenly has a reflex twitch and consequently disrupts your sleep - I would have slept smoothly for another hour or two.

I could hear muffled voices arguing and if my stupid door had been left ajar then maybe I could have made sense of it. Seeing that there were only three people in the house, it had to be Uncle Raj and Mira having a wrangle. I wondered if he had told her what had happened last night. Fat chance of that happening. I was hoping that this would all be over, preferably before the dinner party and before I came out of my room.

I sat in bed, texting Ally about the juicy gossip. *News upd8! R. affair with Ana! Caught out by candid camera (me) Hehehe!! Speak sn. Xxx*

When it comes to sending messages, I become really impatient and press all three keys before the options actually appear. Whilst I waited for her reply I went to get myself ready. Her responses were always delayed. Sometimes I would have trouble remembering what message I had originally sent her when she finally replied.

I went and took a hot shower. The en-suite was complete with a frosted-glass look. It was actually rather sensuous, as it produced a silhouette effect from the other side of the glass. I think the jet shower was designed to deliver a head massage whilst having a shower. Needless to say, it was far too powerful for me, especially in the morning. It felt like big droplets of lead falling on my head.

When I was dry, I picked up my phone, which displayed a message symbol on it. So I opened it up only to find a report stating that it had been delivered to all. WHAT!? This couldn't be happening! I needed to be attached to one of those cardiovascular monitors. I was enduring irregular heartbeats, and in fact I'm sure that I skipped a few. Shit, shit, shit!

My impatience had cost me dear; I had just informed everyone of something relating to Uncle Raj that I wasn't even considering telling his own wife. I might as well have broadcast it live on air. Oh my God! I didn't know what to do. Being in such a frenzy of panic, I was having trouble recalling exactly what I had put in that stupid text message. The harder I tried to remember, the more vague the message was becoming.

Turning on the radio, I sat on the bed with a towel wrapped around me wondering how the hell I could blag myself out of this pile of shit I had landed in, and what I could say to the people who got the message. It had obviously been sent to people with whom I no longer kept in touch, but whose numbers I had forgotten to erase, acquaintances with whom it might be useful to stay in touch with for job purposes, and most importantly uncles, aunts and cousins who were more directly affected by this family scandal.

Trying to look on the bright side of life I thought that this unfortunate incident might lead to a more fortunate result. One of my acquaintances might be able to get me a job writing for the gossip column of a sleazy newspaper. I guess you have to start somewhere.

Ready to be bombarded with text messages asking for more details, I got dressed and decided to seek advice from Ally herself to see if she could suggest anything. So I gave her a call. I had no time to start off the conversation with a general chit-chat about life, so I got straight down to the nitty-gritty:

'Hey, you won't believe what I've just done,' I said.

'Now let me think . . . someone as stupid as you probably sent the message to someone else instead of me'. My god, she knows me far too well, I thought. If we ever became enemies, then I would be in serious trouble.

'I did worse than that, I accidentally sent the goddamn message to everyone,' I told her shakily.

'You knobhead,' she grunted, making me feel even worse than I already did. In my defence, I started to complain and moan about why my phone even had that stupid option in the first place. After allowing me to ramble on for a while, she interrupted:

'Don't stress, they won't understand it anyway,' she said.

'What do you mean?' I responded bewilderedly.

'Well, firstly you only put his first initial in the text message and secondly you didn't put her real name, did you? You keep calling her Anastacia, so unless everyone else knows your little secret code-names they are gonna have no idea what you're talking about!'

I was so relieved I gave her a huge kiss over the phone. I remembered why she was my best friend, because she always puts things into perspective for me. Thanks to her, I felt so much better. An enormous smile reappeared on my face. I stood up and started miming my favourite tune that was playing on the radio. As if that wasn't enough, I was so happy I began to dance wildly around the room – something you do when not in the company of others.

Suddenly, I heard a door slam shut. I wasn't sure which of the two had left the house, but was hoping it was Uncle Raj. Just then, Mira knocked on my door and entered the room. What was the point of knocking if she was not going to wait for a response? I managed to stop prancing around and acted like I was packing my things away, just in the nick of time.

Anyway, she sat on the edge of the bed and the two corners of her mouth were forced into an upward curl, almost but not quite producing a smile. She had obviously come to talk about something a little more serious than my wacky dance moves.

In a soft voice she asked whether I had had a good night's sleep. I knew then that she knew that I knew what had happened. I jumped into the deep end and mentioned that I had heard Uncle Raj come in late last night.

Tears began to trickle down her face and I didn't get a chance to continue.

'This has been going on for so long but who can I tell?' she sobbed.

Just because I had studied 'counselling youth offenders' as part of my degree, I hoped she didn't think I was a marriage counsellor too. I wanted to help but didn't know how, so I suggested going to Relate, or to consult someone else. That did not go down too well, however. I had forgotten that Asians keep family problems within the family. I did not dare to mention the big 'D' word. Divorce is frowned upon in our community and is not really an option in any circumstances. I asked her if there was anything I could do, but her only response was to plead with me not to tell anyone about it. Thank God she did not know about the text message. I agreed weakly, and we had breakfast and continued preparing for the party. As time passed,

I was hoping that the tension would ease up and Uncle Raj would be home in time for the celebration.

People were supposed to be arriving at about half past six. What that really meant was that they would start to turn up at around half past seven. That is not due to being fashionably late but better known as 'Indian timing'. Despite yesterday's tropical heat, the day was looking miserable, and it wasn't long before the drizzle outside turned into heavy rain. Later that afternoon, Uncle Raj came in drenched as a rat. He headed straight upstairs without saying a word to either of us. Hmm, they were having a party to celebrate their anniversary; however, neither of them was talking to the other. It was going to be an entertaining night.

By the time we had finished making snacks and dips for the party, we had only half an hour or so to change our clothes. Mira set the dinner table with their finest cutlery that was yet to be christened. The gold-rimmed plates and sparkling crystal glasses were still wrapped up in tissue paper and were kept in a wooden case. For every plate Mira placed on the table, Uncle Raj replaced it with a plastic one. Standing well out of their way, all I was hoping for was that they would postpone their domestic feud. I felt disconcerted, and escaped into the kitchen. Uncle Raj said that the dinner-set was not dishwasher-friendly and he didn't want Mira to spend most of the night cleaning up. She didn't argue, just put them away. He had used that as an excuse, because I was there. We all knew what it came down to; he was a stingy miser who didn't want everyone to make use of the dinner-set.

A few people arrived, none of whom I knew. They were speaking amongst themselves so I left them to it, and like a coward stayed in the kitchen feigning involvement with the preparation of the food. My parents, Uncle Amir and Auntie Seema arrived together. My cousins followed them into the house. I never thought the day would dawn when I would be glad to see them, one of them in particular - Ana. She looked down her nose as she walked past me and headed straight into the kitchen. Vanessa had cleverly used revision as a viable excuse for not going to these social events and parties and it worked every time.

The food had been put into ceramic dishes ready to be warmed up in the oven. The spicy duck curry was the first to go in. The women were all huddled in the kitchen and the men were sitting in the living room talking about work, cars and other boyish things whilst drinking whisky, brandy and other spirits. Naturally something kept attracting me to that room - no, not their ever so stimulating discussion, nor was it the alcohol. This time it was because there was an exceptionally stunning guy whom I had not seen before sitting in the room, not really contributing to the topic of conversation. I kept popping in and out of the room, but no one had the decency to introduce me to him.

A big square cake topped with fresh fruit and whipped cream had been placed on the table. Everyone seemed to be enjoying themselves. Uncle Raj and Mira were doing a good job of concealing their problems. However, they were keeping their distance from each other.

Finally, dinner was to be served. I went to get the spicy duck curry out of the oven and oh, sweet Moses, the view was not a pretty one. Some twat (that would be me) had left the plastic cover on the dish. Oh crap, what was I thinking? See - that's what happens when I am instructed to do too many things at once. I forgot to take the clingfilm off before I placed it in the oven. Now the duck really would taste rubbery!

The plastic had only half-melted into the curry but it was definitely inedible. If my mother ever found out, I would have a life membership for shadowing her in the kitchen. Then she would kill me. So I was planning on keeping it to myself.

So, should I identify myself as the culprit? I didn't even notice the cover in the first place...I wasn't sure whether to confess or to save myself by claiming anonymity. I thought it was best to choose the latter option. This was where my acting skills came into play. I took the 'rubber duck' out of the oven, and with my eyebrows slightly raised and mouth a tad open, I successfully demonstrated the 'shock look'. Suddenly everyone's eyes were directed towards the oven. No one was quite sure what to say.

Mira was trying to figure out what to do. Everyone started to blame each other about who had put the curry into the oven but kept their voices down. One of the ladies thought she would give Sherlock Holmes a run for his money, so she started to go back over what everyone had been assigned to do. I didn't know who she was, but her strong leadership qualities and her screechy voice set her in a league of her own. The 'big mama' took up most of the space in the kitchen as well as dominating the situation. It was only when she started accusing others that people's voices bagan to rise. I did not realise that such an issue would lead to disarray, and innocent people were being blamed for something I had done. The arguments were creating a division between the group of women in the kitchen.

I raised my voice slightly, hoping that no one would actually pay any attention to me. But all the ladies stopped squabbling and listened to what I was about to confess.

'Okay, look it was me who left the cover on the dish. It was purely an accident and let's not make such a big deal out of it.'

Silence aired the room. I felt pleased that I had owned up and stopped what could have become quite a brawl that evening. It was funny, the way things went back to normal, as if nothing had happened, within minutes of my 'guilty' plea. Everyone carried on with their duties and I could hear three old witches, one of them Uncle Raj's mother, complaining about how I had ruined the party. Luckily, I was not in the right frame of mind to be ruthless; otherwise I could have given her a heart attack if I had mentioned what her son had really been up to.

The Indian Sherlock Holmes seemed to be rather mystified that she had been pointing the finger at the wrong person and therefore decided to claim that I was lying and should not take the blame for someone else's actions. She justified her point by arguing that there was absolutely no way an intelligent girl with a degree would make such a mistake. Do these women live in the real world or have I unknowingly entered the 'matrix'? I was flattered, but my so-called degree was actually becoming a bit of a nuisance for, not only was it not attracting any jobs but it had put an awful lot of pressure on me by insinuating that I could do no wrong. However, her statement was taken offensively by the 80 per cent of non-graduates in the kitchen. This was about to stir up trouble yet again. I had done my bit, I was not going to admit to my mistake for the second time, but I was definitely going to use this 'reverse psychology' technique more regularly.

The discussion became heated yet again and my cousin Driz put in her tuppence-worth. 'Yeah man, jus' 'cos we ain't degree people' (I think she meant graduates) 'it don't mean we're fick.' Trying to maintain a straight face and not involve myself in the discussion, I heard the three old gossip bags chattering amongst themselves. They were talking so loudly it was hard not to listen, especially when their conversation involved my name in it. They were convincing each other that I would not have done a stupid thing like that, and applauded my bravery in claiming responsibility. One minute they were accusing me of wrecking the party, the next they were praising me for taking the blame. Like a light switch, they would just as easily turn on and off by either supporting someone or turning against them, depending on the majority decision.

Like a chairman overseeing a debate, Mira interrupted and

said that there was to be an end to this discussion. The damage was done and it could not be rectified. Nevertheless there were other things that needed to be seen to. At that moment, more people entered the house and made themselves at home. I'm sure some of them only came to eat the food that Mira and I had been slaving over for hours.

Everything was ready and set out on the table. The cake had been cut and gifts were being presented to the couple from all directions. Uncle Raj made a speech. He said he was the happiest man ever. (That was because he had two women, one with whom to practise his kama sutra positions and the other to clean his dirty laundry!) He glanced over at me and then towards Ana, and, continuing with his unprepared speech, he thanked everyone for attending and helping them celebrate the joyous occasion. All I could think about was the food. I was starving.

As always, the men sat down to have dinner and the women served the food. I felt like a bloody waitress. They were talking like there was no tomorrow. I really wanted to tell them to shut up and quickly finish eating but had to resist the temptation. After all, they had only just started feasting.

There were many people there for what was supposed to be a small dinner party. I couldn't begin to think how many guests you'd have to invite for a big dinner party. Meanwhile, things had settled down in the kitchen and two small groups had formed. The parents were at one end and the youngsters at the other. The latter had this tendency to shout over each other, so not only could we hear what they were gossiping about, but I'm sure the rest of the world could too. Ana, Driz and Drin were wearing black trousers and long-sleeved frilly tops, – probably the only half-decent tops they owned. The worst thing was, they were all wearing exactly the same style of clothing with a slight variation in colour. They even wore exactly the same pointed boots.

I should have informed them that the women in the clothes catalogue usually model the same garments in different colours so that people can see the different types of shades on show, not because it's a fashion trend! Now all they had to do was wear the sombreros and they would be The Three Amigos! I made small talk with them, then spoke to the other girls who were a little more interesting.

My attention was drawn towards the conversation at the other side of the kitchen, which was far more engaging.

'You know I was looking out of the window, just watching the cars go by, and I saw about three boys go into Asha's house at different times,' the Indian Sherlock Holmes said.

'Childeren are becoming naughtier day by day. Just recently I heard about an Indian girl having an affair with a married man.' It is better to get them married early, don't you think, Bhindu?'

'Oh yes, definitely.'

Finally the men had finished feeding their faces and nobody had even realised that the spicy duck curry dish was missing. When they went back into the living room to have a few more drinks and a smoke, it was our turn at last. They had taken so long eating the food, that just before we sat down, we had to reheat it all again. I kept well away from the dishes that needed to go in the oven, for obvious reasons.

During the dinner, I immediately set about gobbling my food. I had to force myself to take long pauses in between stuffing my face, so everyone else could catch up. The so-called party was nearly coming to an end. Unfortunately I had never got the chance to speak to the mystery bloke; no one had introduced us. I supposed it was down to serendipity.

And then I thought: why should I let that stop me? I plucked up the courage to go and introduce myself. He was standing near the kitchen doorway, ready to go back into the living room. I planned to speak to him without him knowing that I was trying to make an effort. I got closer and closer and could not think of a reason that I could use to speak to him so I decided to simply introduce myself and just go with the flow.

Then I became timid and remembered the days when I was thirteen and tried asking the teacher I fancied to explain the homework he had set for us. At that exact moment, Auntie Sherlock Holmes tried to squeeze between me and the other side of the doorframe. I was still not aware of her real name; as for the 'Auntie' bit - well, we call everyone who is part of the older generation Aunts or Uncles. It's an Indian thing.

The manoeuvre was like trying to force a suitcase through a letterbox; basically it was never going to happen. Even if she had been a skinny little runt, there was no way she would have been able to pass by without asking me to move. She was far too busy asking 'Deepak' if he was okay. If Auntie Sherlock had concentrated more on asking me to step aside instead of letting the flabby Michelin tyres around her stomach and her bouncy castle-arse just shove me out of the way, I would not have invaded 'Deepak's' personal space or stepped on his foot with my almost-stiletto killer heels. I could see the painful expression he was trying to conceal, which made me feel even worse.

Too embarrassed to say anything but, 'Sorry,' I quickly moved further away. Then I turned back. 'I'm really sorry,' I said again. 'It was that stupid idiotic woman who didn't have the decency to say "Excuse me".'

'Who? My mum!' he chuckled.

Fuuuuuuuuuuuuuuuuuuuuckk! Luckily I only called her a stupid idiot. I think I would have been six feet under, actually probably ready to be cremated if I had said what I really thought of her.

This was not a good start. I decided it would be best to walk away and pretend that I was going to the bathroom. His cheeky smile and effortlessly trendy look was the attraction. However, there was something about him that didn't quite add up.

Annoyingly I couldn't put my finger on it.

We left the party with the majority of the other guests. I sat in the car wondering how many other people are in 'dead end' relationships and are doing nothing about it. What are their reasons? Are they scared to leave or is it the thought of not finding anyone else, because that can prove to be difficult too. And I'm speaking from personal experience here! At the moment I have got plenty to think about and sort out, like finding a job, a man (preferably a rich man, then maybe finding a job would be less of a priority), planning a holiday and starting a health regime…or at least thinking about starting one.

I was going to need more than a dose of luck to sort out my life. This weekend had been an eye-opener for me. It was not that I was naïve, but I never thought that something like this could happen to someone I knew. It was difficult being an Indian wife. Preparing the dinner, looking after the kids, doing the housework and looking over everything else that required attention. If Mira had given a quarter of her dutiful tasks to Uncle Raj maybe he would not have amused himself in other ways.

10

Pinch me . . . I think I'm Dreaming!

I had nothing to look forward to for the rest of the week. It is a well-known phrase or saying that time seems to go quicker when you are having fun. Well, I can tell you that time also flies by when you're doing nothing. On Monday I had created a 'to do' list for the rest of the week. This involved looking for real, attainable jobs and filling out a few application forms, going to sign on at the Job Centre, watching a five-minute update of what task the group had been allocated in the Big Brother house on TV and also finding time to go and see what Ally was doing.

Most of my other friends lived too far away for them to meet up with me during the day. They resided in Scotland, France and a tiny village that could almost be classified as non-existent somewhere near Cornwall. The rest of my friends were either travelling or working. So, my playmate for most of the time was the ever-reliant Ally.

A few days had passed and disappointingly, only one out of the five things had been crossed off my list. And that was only because I had to go and sign on or I would not have got my money for the fortnight. I had no idea what I had been doing for the rest of the time. It felt like every time I blinked, it was tomorrow, and I would still be where I started off. Time-management was the answer - but how to do it was the question.

I pondered on that thought while I texted Kieran to see if he was still alive. Kieran is half Indian and half English. During our school years, he would get teased by the other children about this. This often resulted in fights, which got him into a lot of trouble. After dropping out of school at the age of sixteen, he found an office job and has worked his way up the ladder to become a risk assessor for an insurance company. Like his father, Kieran has a tendency to date Asian women and most of his relationships end within a matter of days. Admittedly some of his girlfriends were on a 'no strings attached' basis. I liked him but wasn't sure if anything would come of it; we were two very different people. I know opposites attract but there has to be some common ground in the first place. On the minus side, the boy lacked common-sense and spoke street lingo that I found difficult to grasp. On the plus side, he was a good kisser, and very attractive.

I didn't particularly want a trophy boyfriend on my arm, yet I was sure that he wanted a 'Tim, nice but dim' girlfriend who would do everything he asked her to do. (Yeah, you still do get these dumb bimbos who fall at a man's feet even in this day and age.) So after that one-off kiss, we tacitly agreed just to be friends, but I hoped the odd snog was not totally out of the picture. On the rare occasions I went round to his house, after a ten-minute chat we always ended up playing games on his PlayStation 2. So, when it came to finding myself a mister, I was back to square one.

Before I went to meet Ally, I decided to surf the net for the supposedly billions of jobs that were on offer. I was no expert at using this thing and therefore kept clicking the links in order to progress. I knew there was a way of permanently getting rid of the annoying pop-up messages that kept appearing on the screen but even after half an hour spent trying to find out how to go about it, I was still unsuccessful.

I also started to get instant chat messages from a weirdo who was being rather obscene. I couldn't understand how the hell my name and a false profile of me had been created. I had not made one, because I would not know where to start. As they kept reappearing after I had closed down the window, I thought the best way to get rid of them would be to reply to the message. I clicked on the guy's profile and read the following:

Screen name: Screwman
Age: ????
Hobbies: Cars and chicks.
Marital status: Sort of single
Extra info: Keep it real!

Oh my goodness, what a complete psycho. I'll give him what for, I thought. I asked him his age. He chose to ignore that question and asked for mine. I said fourteen years old. He started to make suggestive comments and I was fazed by how easy it was for dirty, filthy old men to talk to little girls in such a lewd manner.

I thought that since I had entered a false age, he would find someone his own age to talk dirty to. However, I was completely mistaken. I ignored his message, but he kept persisting, sending more, describing what he would like to do to me. Ugh! That's it, I thought to myself. I sent him a message saying that this was a police operation tracking down people who used the Internet to lure girls under the age of sixteen. We had in fact identified him and were coming to get him. At which point there was no response from him and when I went to send him another message, he had already logged off! (Probably crapping himself!)

If I had not created this profile then it could only have been Vanessa. So this is what she gets up to when she tells my parents she is revising. I was preparing to kill her when she returned home from her friend's house for making a profile using my name. I didn't have to wait long before I heard her open the front door and walk up the stairs to her room.

'Vanessa!' I shouted. She put her bag down and came into my room.

'What?' she said, looking rather tired.

'Did you use the chat-room service with my profile?' I interrogated. She paused and knew that there was no point lying about it.

'I was only messing around, Neen. I know I shouldn't have used your name, it was stupid of me. Sorry.'

I knew that she was stressed out about her exams, and I didn't have the heart to ramble on about the dangers of using chat-rooms. Mind you, the gimp probably knew much more than I did about the world of surfing. I told her about my experience using the chat-messaging thing and she checked through the different profiles for me, to see if *Screwman* was still there because I didn't know how to do it. No surprises that the screen name no longer existed. It really was amazing to see how quickly it disappeared. Even though his profile name and description had probably just changed to another one. I lay on my bed for forty winks before I went round to Ally's house.

Vanessa was still surfing the net when my phone started to ring. I answered the call, and it was Ally. She insisted that I run to her house because she had something important to tell me. She was trying to contain her excitement over the phone. It could only be that Dylan had finally done what everyone was waiting for and proposed. I was not in the least bit surprised but would have to pretend I was gob-smacked when she told me. Although I was immensely happy for them, I couldn't help but wonder when it would be my turn.

When I turned the corner of her street, I could see her waiting outside, making urgent hand gestures to hurry up. I got to the door, and I was welcomed with a great big bear hug. I could see she was bursting to tell me something. She made me play the guessing game. I tried to think of a piece of news that didn't involve Dylan's proposal, so I guessed that she had found a job, which was most unlikely, considering that she had not really applied for any. Knowing that the answer would be 'no', I begged her to just tell me.

'You are never gonna believe this, Neen,' she assured me, while she let me in the house and then raced up the stairs to her bedroom. She leaped on the bed. I sat on the chair, stomping my feet and insisting that she tell me the news. After catching her breath, she gazed at me with sparkling eyes. 'I won that competition. We're going to India - you and me - next week! AAAARRRRGGGHHHHH!!!!!!!!!!!!!!!

In my usual manner, I nearly fell off the chair when she finally told me. I have not been so pleasantly surprised since the time I received my A level results; I did shit-all work for them and still ended up with A,B,B while in the meantime I had been thinking that I would have to repeat the year. *But this was ten times better than that.* I had thought that most competitions were scams; a complete waste of time.

Ally told me she had received a phone call about two hours ago stating that she had won the first prize for that competition she had entered a week ago in *Fashion* magazine. The best thing was, she had chosen *me* to go with her! The tickets would arrive in a few days and we were to leave in a week's time. Ally had decided to opt for the celebrity makeover, which included tickets to attend the movie awards ceremony in India for her and a friend.

'Ally, you're a genius,' I burbled excitedly. 'Oh my God, I can't believe we are going to India.'

'I can't believe it either' said Ally. 'We better start packing,' she continued.

We needed to sort everything out and we only had a week. I wanted to tell my parents, therefore needed to get home as quickly as possible. In desperation, I called a taxi. I was not thinking straight and soon realised that the waiting time for the damn thing would be longer than just going home by foot. So off I went, being extra cautious on the roads. I wouldn't want to get run over now. Apart from missing the holiday, I was wearing Bridget Jones-style big knickers.

I was rushing home, my mind in a whirl: the whole thing had not sunk in yet. I was going to India for the first time, for two weeks, staying in the best hotels and being chauffeured in a limousine and, of course, being treated just like a celebrity. I raced into the house, shouting, 'Hey, guess what! I'm going to India!' but no one was in. I was desperate to tell everyone and anyone. So the next best thing was to call all my friends who would be green with envy that they were slaving away at a desk in order to be able to afford a week's break in Europe while I was jetting off to the Asian continent for absolutely free.

I made a list of all the things I needed. I would take two suitcases, one for shoes and the other for clothes. Ally and I apparently had five hundred pounds each in spending money too, which I'm sure, when converted into rupees, would amount to about a million - okay, maybe a little less than that - 40,000 rupees. I wasn't sure what to do, but I felt like I needed to do something. Waiting for my parents to return home was so frustrating. Where could they have gone? They hardly ever go out unless it's food shopping. Most of that is done in bulk, which lasts a good couple of months.

Just as I was about to explode like a whistling kettle, the parents arrived.

'Mum! Dad!' I gabbled, the minute they got in the door. 'You won't believe this - I'm going to India!' I told them that Ally had entered a competition and had won a trip to India.

After twenty billion questions about who else was going, what type of competition she had entered, how long and whereabouts we would be staying in India and what we would be doing, my dad said to be careful and look after my belongings. The only reason this trip had not become an issue was because it was a freebie.

My mother could not understand why she had never been lucky enough to win anything when she entered competitions. It could have been because she only entered those catalogue competitions where they state that the addressee has been selected to win a hundred thousand pounds and is through to the next stage. To qualify they must send the response back in the pre-paid envelope within fourteen days.

Out came the phone diary and my mum started to call my aunts and uncles to inform them of the news. Usually when they go to India, people in this country take various items to give to their relatives over there. It did not click with me that this might be the reason why Mum had phoned all of them. When she told me that everyone was coming round to our house with gifts for me to deliver to their relatives, I wanted to throttle her.

If I wanted to deliver post or gifts for people, then I would have worked for Royal Mail or UPS! If it was our relatives then it would not be so bad, but there was no way I was going to give something to someone I didn't even remotely know. Why the hell couldn't these people use Parcel Force or take the blasted things when they went themselves.

Instead of causing a fiasco by standing my ground and saying that I would not do it, I said that this trip was already planned by the organisers and we were only going to Mumbai and the capital, New Delhi. The phone book came out again. When she phoned back to tell them that I was only visiting those two specific cities, they all said that they didn't actually have time to come and visit...the cheeky sods.

'We shall discuss your sightseeing, Nina,' said my dad, who was almost as excited as me, and dead eager to take up the role of a tour guide. He mentioned places that definitely had to be on the viewing list, such as the great Taj Mahal and the castle remains that dated back to the Mogul years when India was under British rule. He was about to continue, then stopped and said it would be easier to discuss this when I received the itinerary for the two weeks. This all seemed surreal. I kept thinking that Ally was playing a practical joke on me or that there had been some sort of mistake when selecting the winner. After all, she'd had nothing in writing. My heart sank at the thought that it might be some cruel joke.

'I hope your passport is still valid,' my father remarked, and I jolted back to the present.

I shot up the stairs so that I was breathless when I got to the top. Everything always went stupidly wrong for me, and if it wasn't all a horrible mistake, then this was it – an invalid passport. I had not used it for such a long time.

With trembling hands, I dug deep into my drawer, which was heaped with my unopened bank statements and other unwelcome things that had been thrown in there as soon as they came through the letterbox. I was waiting for them to file themselves away in a folder containing dividers that I had created when I was going through an 'organising frenzy' phase, but they were too lazy.

Ah ha. Found it! I snatched it open and breathed a sigh of relief on finding it was still valid for another eight months, but there was absolutely *no way* I was showing that bloody passport pic to anyone. I must have had that photo taken when I was about fourteen. I wished someone had combed my hair for me before they stuck me in that photo booth. My hair was an Afro, and there was lots of untamed bitty hair that could not be tied up into my ponytail. As for eyebrows, well, there should have been two and preferably a little bit thinner and my teeth were definitely an example of the before and after effect, thanks to the invention of braces.

Come to think of it, the only reason I escaped being bullied at school was because everyone else looked similar and wore the same outfits. Anyone who grew up in the 1980s was a complete and utter fashion victim. Shell-suits and big hairdos are nowadays considered to be so dire, that if parole violators were made to wear them as part of their punishment then I think they would be too emotionally distressed to re-offend. I was not looking forward to Security checking my passport. It was going to be a really embarrassing moment.

As soon as Ally received the fax containing the itinerary, she posted a copy through the letterbox while driving past my house. As my passport was still valid, I had thought I had nothing to worry about. That was until the word 'visa' was brought to my attention.

Visa - what's that? But I'm British, I don't need visas. I never had to get them when I went travelling two years ago. I informed my dad, who shook his head and looked rather worried that he had created such an idiot of a daughter.

'That was because you went to Europe.' He sighed deeply; 'I am so glad Alisha is going with you.'

'Will you come with me to get the visa, please, Dad?' I asked piteously. I didn't feel up to doing it on my own. The only reason anyone would consider going anywhere with their parents voluntarily is because they didn't know how to cope with something themselves.

'Why can't you go by yourself? I'm not going to take a day off work just so I can come with you - or won't you be able to find it?' he said condescendingly.

Damn. 'I'm not stupid you know,' I said crossly. 'Of course I'll find it.'

At the end of the day, how difficult can obtaining a visa actually be? On the website, I found the address and a few handy tips about the information they required. They also advised people to arrive at the Indian High Commission as early as possible.

Although Ally was as hopeless as me and would be of little help, I was hoping that we could go and get the visas together. Safety in numbers and all that. Using the old method of telecommunication, I gave her a bell. Unfortunately her visa from a former trip was still valid, which left the onus on me. I became more and more apprehensive as I still wasn't exactly clear about what I was actually supposed to do when I got there.

The next morning arrived much faster than anticipated. My parents gave me directions to the Indian High Commission office. Apparently it was situated in Aldwych. I was to go to that station and then head towards the BBC. That should be easy enough.

Off I went with my little red book and a much more recent photo, but just as unflattering as the other one, to Maida Vale station. Seeing the mile-long queue at the ticket window, I stood in line to purchase a ticket from the automated machine. The incompetent machine was not accepting notes, so I searched for my silvers and golds (which were made up of coppers), browsed to find 'Chancery Lane' station and then pressed the button, waiting for a sign to tell me to insert the money. I hit the button again, and again and again. A long queue was starting to form behind me. I think the bloody machine had frozen. All the City businessmen who had parked their arses behind me were huffing and puffing, wondering why I was taking so long.

I had to be the one to break the bad news. Don't be silly, not to everyone, just the person behind me. Then she told the person behind her and the domino effect slowly rippled along. I marched off to join the mile-long queue to purchase my ticket from the counter, and the rest of the sheep had no choice but to follow. After waiting for at least twenty minutes, I asked the assistant for a ticket to Chancery Lane station. To this I received the reply that the station was closed. Yet again, the line of agitated and angry people were held up while I found out what the nearest station was to Chancery Lane. That was an absolutely great start to my day. Perfect!

As I walked through the barriers, I glanced back and saw people using the automated ticket machine. Their tickets came out and they were on their way. That's when an irate man shouted, 'Who said that the machine was not working?' so half of the people in the queue went back to joining the original one. I stood behind a pillar to wait for the train, just in case that man recognised me.

The changing of the Underground lines and being sandwiched in between men whose sweat was seeping through their shirts, was making me feel sick. Finally breathing in fresh, albeit polluted air, I made my way out of Holborn station and headed down Kingsway towards Aldwych.

I walked up and down the street and saw no sign of the building. People were brushing past me as they rushed to work. Before I wasted any more time, I had to do the tourist thing and ask for directions, preferably not from another tourist. That was if I could find anyone walking slow enough to stop. Every time I attempted to grab someone's attention, they would simply walk past as if I was one of those promoters selling special offer products. When I finally managed to arrive at my destination, I understood why I had missed it in the first place. There was no big flag, and no imposing building. The whole place looked modest and had an inconspicuous side entrance down a short flight of steps.

I entered the premises and followed the stairs leading up to the first floor. A large number of people were already waiting there. I had thought I would be one of the first to arrive, but I obviously thought wrong. The place was packed, like a tin of sardines. I noticed that everyone was busy filling out forms, but where did they get them from? More importantly, where was I supposed to get a ticket to join the queue?

The woman beside me must have been telepathic; she said that the forms had to be collected from the small window just outside the office. I was starting to become really fed up. I reversed my arse out of the building and went back outside. Whoever thought of this procedure really needed to get their head checked. There was no shelter for the people waiting in the queue – can you imagine if it was raining or snowing? We would all be soaking wet. I received my form and a ticket displaying the number eighty-four on it. *To be filled out in capitals and black ink*, the form stated. I had no pen, let alone a black one. I could not believe that everyone was rude enough to refuse the loan of their pen when I asked them. Did they really think that I was going to run off with the pen they had nicked from an Argos superstore? I don't think so.

I ended up borrowing a blue pen from an old Sikh because I had given up attempting to find a black one. He was wearing a royal-blue turban and had an extremely long grey-white moustache and beard. Most of his teeth were a stale yellow colour. I tried not to stare, but he reminded me of the man in one of my favourite childhood stories, *The Twits*. I filled out the form as quickly as possible, so I could return his pen and move away. It was going to be a long wait, since they were only calling for number fifty-three. All the seats were occupied and my feet were killing me. If only I had worn flat shoes.

The room was reasonably small and there were seven counters in a row on the left-hand side of the entrance. I counted fifty chairs, all taken, and the remaining people had to find somewhere to stand – preferably not on someone else's toes.

It was almost as if the government had picked up a building from India and simply brought it over to this country and stuck it next to some others in central London. That could be said for the people working there too. They had the 'typical freshie accent' and the whole atmosphere felt foreign. In a strange way, it added to the excitement.

The Sikh was looking over my shoulder, so I tried to hide the information by covering most of the form with my hand. Even after I gave him his pen back, he was lingering around me like a bad smell. I hoped he wasn't expecting a favour in return! There was no air-conditioning, and the walls were showing signs of damp - or it could have been perspiration from all the people who had been standing against it, leaving a big sweat patch as they walked away. Maybe they were trying to gently warn us that this was the norm in India...disorganised, baking hot and very Third World.

My parents had made a trip to India on numerous occasions, so I had seen what our village was like in photos and a video film. Surely not all parts of India would have holes in the floor to take a shit and a limited supply of electricity that cuts out when it is most needed, would they?

Feeling exhausted, I purchased my visa and bought a bottle of water in case I was thirsty on my way back home.

11
The Magazine Shoot

Two days before the big departure, Ally and I went to have our photos taken. These were to appear in *Fashion* magazine to show the readers who were the lucky ones to have won the trip. We had to take three different outfits and our scary faces (without make-up) to the studio beneath the magazine offices.

The magazine headquarters were situated near Marble Arch, in a lean, archaic building located out of the way on a side street resembling an alleyway. Rubbish overflowed out of the dustbins all around. I would not have thought for a single minute that people working for such a reputable magazine would be slogging away in a dump like this. The building was decorated with graffiti, which was created in quite a tasteful manner, however the whole place had the air of a derelict site. The pair of us wondered what it would have been like walking through here in the dark and counted our blessings that it was summer. It must be a prime spot for muggers.

Arriving ten minutes before the expected time, we rang the bell. Out came a tall woman with mid-length, tousled blonde hair and a blonde moustache to match. Black leather knee-high boots covered her long legs and her 34HHH bust was practically exposed because her top lacked sufficient material. She spoke to us in German and smiled as she pointed her finger to the spiral metal staircase that led up to the next floor. I instinctively thought that we had got ourselves into something very dodgy. I was expecting the whip to come out if we didn't get up the stairs quickly enough. I mumbled this to Ally but she didn't catch on. The studio was full of bright spotlights and lots of cable wires crossing over one another on the floor. There were various types of cameras and a bed in front of a white screen.

A short man who was also in the studio came over and introduced himself as Stefan. His unwashed denim jeans were held up with a dark brown belt that had been done up a notch too tight, thus enhancing the size of his beer belly. His shirt was unbuttoned from the chest upwards, allowing a full view of his thick, double-twisted gold chain. Prior to shaking hands, he held a large bag of crisps in one hand, while with the other, he licked the crumbs off his grotty fingers and then wiped them on his jeans. His grotesque mannerisms had definitely cured my addiction for crisps. There was absolutely no way I was touching that dirty bugger's hands so I waited for Ally to do it first.

Stefan put his hand out and we both stood there until it became uncomfortable. I nudged Ally and she grudgingly shook his hand. Next, it was my turn. I confirmed that we were here for the magazine shoot and then went to shake his hand. In the nick of time, the bag of crisps fell to the floor and saved me from doom because he was trying to sweep up the mess as he continued to apologise. He said that first we should take a look at the type of shots we would be expected to do. I did not like the sound of this. As he brought the portfolio over he told us to strip. I took a quick glimpse at the photos and every single one of them was nude! I shouted at Ally and questioned her about exactly what type of competition she had entered. She herself was baffled and asked whether they were part of *Fashion* magazine.

'Who? Who are dey?' Stefan kept repeating, as if we didn't hear him the first time. He had never heard of them. We were obviously in the wrong place and made a beeline for the door. The man followed us. 'But you pretty, sexy lookin' gals,' he said, trying to persuade us to do a few shots. 'You could be future stars. I have personal contacts with all the adult channels, including the Playboy production team,' he continued. Holding hands, we ran out and were relieved to see the light of day and breathe the glorious air of freedom.

We phoned *Fashion* magazine on Ally's mobile and walked to their studio while the receptionist gave us directions over the phone. Aha, that was better! This looked more like somewhere a magazine would be produced. It was round the corner from the dingy alley. Confusion arose because it was still classed as being on the same street. They could at least have warned us! Our hearts were still racing and Ally was whispering that she didn't want to do this any more. I did not recollect her saying this when we entered the porn house. Maybe she was in shock (after shaking that man's hand!). I told her to shut up and get a grip, because this was the real thing.

The reception area was spacious and the walls were covered with shots of celebrities who had previously appeared on the magazine cover. The editor, Sarah Patterson, approached us with a warm welcome and said that they would take only two shots of each of us because they were running on a really tight schedule. My excitement was based solely on the fact that I might see a famous person here. I know it's sad, but I would have to get his or her autograph, or else no one would believe me!

As we walked down to the studio, we passed through the office. Everyone had two phones and a flatscreen computer, yet hardly anyone was sitting at their desk. With two phones at hand, I would be glued to my chair, dialling my way through my 'friends and family' phone directory to have a little natter. It would all be work-related, of course. Instead, the staff were all rushing around like headless chickens shouting to one another across the room. The office was modern and clean, with loose sheets of paper left on chairs and desks. The studio was divided into two parts, one of which was the make-up room. There were lots of cable wires cutting across the floor. In a way, it was similar to the studio we had just seen.

The make-up artists were called Christina and Yatunde. Christina had tanned olive skin and her accent indicated that she was from one of the Mediterranean islands. She wore heavy make-up around her hazel eyes, which attracted attention. There was not a single hair out of place. It must have been the hairspray - either that, or she spent most of her day in front of the mirror, perfecting herself. She was wearing a frilly white apron that had been covered with splashes of coloured eye-shadow powder and lipstick marks too.

Yatunde told us she had left Jamaica to come and work in Britain. She was tall, and if her wacky make-up had been toned down a little, then she too would have been very beautiful. She was also suffering from some form of verbal diarrhoea. From the moment we met, she could not stop talking. Ally and I sat beside each other and faced a large mirror. In front of us were billions of different shades and colours of eye-shadow, foundation, blusher etc. Ally got Christina to do her make-up and I got Motor-mouth to do mine. Both girls were boasting about the work they had done with minor celebrities. The super-celebs were apparently always accompanied by their own make-up artist and hairstylist.

'Right, me gonna do you a Jamaic-over,' Yatunde said imposingly with an enormous grin.

I didn't like the sound of this. I saw how much foundation she had ready to slap on to my face and thought it was a good time to give her a few hints as to my requirements. That was when she gave me a chance to talk.

'I usually wear quite subtle colours. I like the natural look,' I mentioned, when I saw her pick up a green eye-shadow.

'You don't want to look natural, for a magazine shoot. People seeya looking natural every day,' she continued, whilst applying that bogey-green colour to my eyelids. 'In Ja-maica da gals have competitions on who can wear da most make-up widout looking like clowns…and guess who won it last year? Me.'

I was horrified. This was not going well. I turned to Ally who was holding in her laugh. Mind you, she was looking just as bad.

The two girls said that they usually had to put double the normal amount of make-up on people because only then would it show up on the photo. Although it was a little over the top, I could handle my eyes being defined with a black eye pencil and bright lipstick on my lips, but it was the blusher that nearly killed me! I could not bear to look in the mirror, but I didn't have the guts to say that I hated it. I looked like a pixie with rosy cheeks and so did Ally.

I would have done a better job doing my own make-up. Nevertheless, we had to keep smiling for the camera. The make-up took longer than the actual photo-shoot and there was no prior showing of the photos. We would have to wait for them to appear in the magazine's next issue.

As soon as we left the building, we dashed into the nearest pub and sat at a corner table. A few of the light bulbs needed replacing and it was generally empty with only a few old men sitting at the bar.

I made a getaway to the toilets while Ally bought cocktails to cheer us up. I used at least half of the loo roll soaked into water to take the shit off. Slowly but surely it was working, but little bits of tissue were also starting to stick to my face. I removed the blusher and lipstick and went back to our table.

Ally pointed out that my cheeks still had lots of blusher on them, but it was not the blusher; my cheeks had turned red from rubbing at them with the tissue.

We sat there drinking a woo-woo cocktail and giggling about where we had originally ended up and whether Stefan was really a 'glamour photographer' or just a phoney. I'm sure the whole set-up was illegal. Unexpectedly we heard thunder and saw a flash of lightning. That was all we needed. The sun was blazing in the morning and by the afternoon it was pouring down with rain. The weather researchers are not doing a good job if they cannot distinguish between 'sunny' and 'rainy'. We had not even brought our jackets because it was so hot in the morning. There was no way I was about to go out in the rain. I wasn't sure if my mascara was waterproof and I didn't have an umbrella. So we sat in the dingy pub and prayed that it would stop soon. Meanwhile, we got another round of drinks in.

By late afternoon the place was becoming livelier. This pub must have done something right to attract lots of men in suits for a drink after work. Apart from us there was only one other girl who set foot in the pub. While Ally popped to the Ladies, I took a quick look at her. It was rather intriguing to see precisely what made her stand out from the rest of us in the pub. She wore baggy trousers, and a T-shirt with slits that had been secured with safety pins. Attached to the top of her trousers were several metal chains that were clipped to a ring hole a few inches away from the other end of the chains.

The tips of her hair spikes were perfected to points sharp enough to use as lethal weapons. Her hair was short with strands of pink dye that was growing out. Surprisingly there were no visible pierced gems - they were probably tucked away in her mouth or under her clothes! However, a distinctive tattoo lay on the side of her neck. It was some sort of writing in a gothic font. I could not read what it said from such a distance.

Anyway, as I was saying, she came in and looked straight at me and smiled. I acknowledged her gesture (I did not want to get beaten up for not smiling back) and therefore reciprocated the action. She sat at the bar having a conversation with the girl serving her a drink. It didn't take a genius to work out that she was a regular.

Just as we were about to leave, a group of buff (I am using street lingo again, so for the people that are slightly out of touch, that means gorgeous, beautiful, sexy) men entered the tavern. I stared in their direction and thought happily to myself that I had found the perfect place to meet young men who were trendy, good-looking and hopefully bright and minted too. The four men took off their jackets, unbuttoned their cuffs and loosened their ties. I think Ally was being sick in the toilets. She had taken so long that I had time to analyse the girl's clothes and even had a few minutes over to check out those guys. I couldn't see them properly, but I was tying to think of a way which involved moving a little closer to them.

When Ally returned, we had to leave. I tried to persuade her to stay a little longer, however my technique was lacking the 'x' factor. She was not interested in my reasons and waited for me to get up. As we walked over to the door, I had to remember to make a mental note of this pub's name because it was a place that I was definitely coming back to after our holiday. I took a good look at the boys, trying not to be too obvious about it – and found I had the perfect reason to go over. It must be my lucky day!

I had thought I would never see him again. After that dinner party, I tried to think of his name but could not recall it for the life of me. So I simply grinned in a friendly way at him as I walked over to say a quick hello. He remembered where we had previously met – thank God – and he introduced himself as Deepak. One of the guys had gone to buy the drinks and the other two chatted to each other. What, I wondered, was the likelihood of me being in this pub, one I would never normally think of going into, and meeting the man of my dreams?

Deepak had a grin on his face. He must have recalled the time I accidentally called his mum a stupid idiot. Oh dear, I hoped he wasn't going to hold that against me for ever. He said that he had not seen me in this pub before. It was a bad chat-up line, but I was willing to waive that one! Then he turned his head to look at Ally.

'I didn't know you were going...' he began, but before he had the chance to finish his sentence I answered eagerly, 'Oh yeah, for two weeks.'

He continued, looking quite amazed, 'What - so your parents were all right about it? I wish I had your courage.'

'Yeah - why wouldn't they be?' I was only going abroad for two weeks, not leaving the country for good, I thought to myself.

I was waiting for him to ask for my number...come on, get a move on! But he seemed to be more interested in my trip than in me. Another glance at Ally and this time while looking at her, he said, 'Are you going with her?'

'Yeah. I was the lucky one - she chose me.'

Conversation was moving slowly. I was about to end it and suggest that we meet up sometime, but while I tried to word it properly in my head before I spat it out, he beat me to it. Not the suggestion of meeting up, but something that was said in the nick of time, before I made myself look like a fool.

'You've probably guessed, but you have to keep it in the dark. My parents don't know and somehow I don't think they will take it as easily as yours did!' I frowned and wondered what the hell he was talking about. Then everything fell into place when he introduced me to his partner, Jamie. No, not his work partner, his lover. He was GAY!! I actually remember thinking at Mira's party that something didn't quite add up with him, but he was far from the homosexual stereotype. I knew instantly that Jamie was gay though. He flapped his hands around throughout the conversation with his co-worker and maintained a bitchy 'whatever' type of attitude.

There had obviously been a huge misunderstanding. One minute he was asking about my trip... Oh shit, wait a minute, how the hell would he have known about it? This was such a *Fawlty Towers* miscommunication. So much so that it could have been scripted to appear on one of the episodes if the series was still running. We were having two totally different conversations, yet all the questions and answers perfectly matched.

I explained myself, and told Deepak that I had been talking about my holiday that Ally had won in a competition. Silly me – I was completely clueless that we were sitting in a gay pub, although I had wondered why the men didn't look at us when we walked in, as with all that make-up we were quite hard to miss! I was not gay, I told Deepak, and Ally was not my lover. We had initially entered the pub to use the loo.

This was a very subtle gay pub. I have been to a few and they always have posters on the wall about the events occurring in the evening, such as drag queens, 'Best gay of the year' and so on. Mind you, if the pub had been packed with people, I'm sure I would have caught on.

The blood had rushed to the surface of Deepak's skin; his face had started to go red all over. I could sympathise; I kept contemplating what would have happened to me if I had asked him out for a drink. My head would have exploded – either that or I would have eaten myself up, I think. He apologised and asked me not to say anything to anyone. Severely depressed, I agreed and left for the station to jump in front of a train. What a complete waste of talent!

As we walked to the station I told Ally what had happened. She found the whole commotion hilarious. However, she did promise me one thing – we would have so much fun on this holiday that all this would be forgotten. Maybe by then it would be, but for the moment, the whole scene was spinning in circles around my head. I felt like running back into the pub and 'bitch slapping' that Jamie. I might have to give Jerry Springer a call so we could have a stage fight and I could beat him to a pulp without being arrested. I can already imagine the title for the show… *'You made my dream lover GAY!'*

All the excitement about the trip had drained away. Instead my head was filled with dejected thoughts. It was funny how the start of a conversation between two people could lead to them talking about two different things. I had come to an irrational conclusion. The beautiful, sexy, intelligent, funny, rich men (considering that they are scarce to start off with) are either taken or most likely to bat for the other side.

Oh well, shit happens and life goes on. I consoled myself by insisting that I didn't like him that much anyway, and decided that tomorrow was going to be the start of a good day. I could vouch for that one because it was going to involve only one human (myself) and two suitcases. Yes, I'm talking about packing. Hurray!

The next morning I was ready to roll. It took very little time for the excitement to re-enter my system. A cup of Nescafé boosted my adrenaline levels and for once I knew what I needed to pack and the things I was going to take with me. I was simultaneously packing an outfit in one suitcase and then the shoes in another. The job was tiring. Halfway through I took a break and phoned Ally to check what she was packing.

Her packing had already been done. She said it was easier to decide what to pack when they put restrictions on how much you could take. I was going to kill her for not mentioning that we were only allowed to take one suitcase. This proved to be difficult, as I had to reduce everything by half. After a wise decision to take just one pair of shoes that could be worn with most of my outfits, I finally managed to get it all into one suitcase. I had to sit on it to close the damn thing, and even when securely locked, the suitcase had abnormal bulges appearing from the sides. At any minute it was going to burst open, but I was willing to take that chance. India - here we come!

12
The Journey Begins…

Ally's house was the pick-up point. As we waved goodbye to our families and got into the mini-cab that was dropping us at the airport, my parents acted like they were never going to see me again. Maybe they knew something I had yet to find out! Before we started our journey, the ultimate ticket and passport check had to be done. Finally we were leaving bland London and heading for spicy India.

I couldn't believe that we were on our way to the Asian continent. I had been saying that I needed a holiday and now that I had got one, I was going to make the most of it. As soon as we arrived at Heathrow, we queued to check in and then had hours to spare before departure time. So, where better to go than the duty-free shops? It was a good thing too, as it reminded me that I had forgotten to pack my perfumes. We went inside a mini-version of a hypermarket and then split up. Ally headed for the booze and fags and I zoomed over to the perfumes. I wanted everything! In my excitement, I grabbed about six bottles of various fragrances and stuck them in my basket.

I already had trouble with my storage facilities so four of them went straight back on the shelf. Time flew by and I still couldn't decide between two perfumes. Check-in time had been announced. Ally picked one out of my basket and replaced it on the shelf as she pushed me to the payment counter. She went to pay for her booze, fags and her favourite Chanel perfume and the assistant informed her that she needed a licence to convey liquor into India. So the alcohol went back to its original home on the shelf. We spent just over two hours in that store, which meant we had no time to explore some of the neighbouring shops because our flight was about to depart.

It was going to be a very long journey. I had already planned what I was going to do…sleep. We were directed to our seats. Ally and I fought over who was going to sit nearest to the window. After emotionally blackmailing me by saying that she had won the holiday so she should get first choice, I chose to back down.

The airline was one that I had not heard of before. The aeroplane appeared to be as good as new. I hoped that we were not being used as guinea pigs to see if the plane had any faults for its first long-haul flight. It was a tad bigger than the local chartered flights but it had a different layout compared to the normal jumbo jets.

Aeroplane seats are usually closely grouped and just about tolerable – almost similar to the ones you see in cinemas. But these were different because they had a considerable amount of legroom between each row. Even with my legs stretched right out I could not touch the seat in front – and I was wearing three-inch heels. This was fantastic; my bum only took up half of the very spacious seat. The other seats did not appear to be like this one. I thought that we must have got these seats because Ally had won the competition. The stewardesses all looked very similar. They wore their long black hair tied back and had welcoming smiles on their faces. Their uniform consisted of a plain red sari with a black border.

I wanted to know why a few of the back seats were so much more spacious than the rest of them so I asked the stewardess who was standing nearby. She informed me that this airline catered for all types of people. Her subtle point didn't quite register into my brain so I asked her what she meant by that.

'AmerIndia Airlines is a brand new airline owned by an American company,' she said. 'As you can see, it is a standard aircraft with no first-class or business-class seating. However, these newly built planes are designed to cater for the fuller figures of American passengers who wish to travel with this airline.'

'Basically, what she's saying is that these seats are for fatsos who cannot squeeze their arses into the normal-sized ones,' Ally summarised.

'But that's being sizist,' I said.

'Well the Americans don't think so. Anyway, no one complains about a company being "disablist" when they have special seats for those people, do they?'

I could see the point she was trying to make but her ability to invent words and make them sound as though they actually existed made me laugh. The magazine had lied to us. What they classified as first-class seats, actually meant sitting in these ones. Oh I get it, so a heavily overweight person's chair is considered to be economy class when they make use of it, but as soon as a person one eighth of his or her size uses the seat, it is known as 'first-class'! Where's the fairness in that? Nevertheless, I was extremely comfortable and was hoping to sleep throughout most of my journey.

The majority of passengers were Asian, with a few exceptions, and everyone was talking so loudly that we missed the announcement. The captain came out, introduced himself and the co-pilot, and then went back into the cockpit ready for take-off. The plane started to move and everyone cheered. Suddenly, it came to an abrupt halt. It started moving again, there was a trickle of applause, but then two seconds later, the bloody thing was at a standstill again.

'Attention all passengers, we are having a technical difficulty. Once it has been rectified we will depart. Sorry for the delay.'

I was more excited about having to evacuate the aircraft by sliding down the yellow chute. I've always wanted to do that. Fifteen minutes felt like fifteen hours and everyone had to exit the plane. I was pissed off that the opportunity had arisen to use the slide and yet we still had to use the stairs. Our trip had been delayed by almost two hours. The woman sitting in the same row on the seat adjacent to us in the plane, also sat next to us in the departure area that we had to return to. It was not her that I was worried about, it was her kid who was running around causing distress to other people by pulling the labels off their hand luggage. God help us!

Finally all the passengers made their way back into the plane and sat in their seats. The silence was an instant giveaway that everybody was fed up and just wanted to reach their destination. However, they managed to give a huge burst of applause when the plane finally did start moving without having a break in between. As the aircraft headed for the runway, I leaned over to Ally's side to look out of the window and could not help but overhear the conversation between a teenage girl and her dad, who were sitting in front of us. Her dad was enquiring as to why she was not clapping. With a major attitude and a kiss of the teeth, she looked at him and said that she didn't have to do everything that he did. 'They don't deserve a clap,' she carried on.

'Why are you being like this?'

'Okay, fine, if it makes you happy then … there!' With one hand using only her index finger and thumb, she made a clapping gesture. 'In my opinion it definitely didn't deserve a full clap!' she barked. The girl was a spoiled brat who needed a good kick up the backside.

I was nearly crying with laughter. The girl turned around and gave me a dirty look before continuing to give her dad a hard time. I was ready to slap her back to London or wherever she came from as she was starting to become a real nuisance with her constant whinging. The little boy in the next aisle was fidgeting and already pissing off the people who were sitting in front of him with his mischievous tricks. He was so annoying! Why couldn't his mum just tape him to his seat? My tiredness had disappeared but after an hour of being in the air, Ally was starting to drift off. I kept myself busy by reading and listening to my CDs and singing along to the music.

I was bored and there was no one to talk to. I didn't want to scare the other people by talking to myself, so I resorted to closing my eyes and going to sleep for a while.

It was pitch black outside and there was an unsettled feeling in my stomach. It could possibly have been hunger pangs so I put a boiled sweet into my mouth to keep me going for a bit and also to prevent my ears from being blocked by the change in air pressure. As soon as I swallowed the sweet, I fell asleep, expecting to awake to the smell of nice hot food.

Ally had been asleep for nearly four hours and I do not remember her getting up at any point for any reason. I had been sleeping for three hours but during that time I had to get up on numerous occasions. Once I had to go to the loo. Then the 'dad' in front of us started to snore really loudly, which disrupted my sleep and also his, because his daughter elbowed him in the stomach. After that, I felt something hit my neck and had to check what the hell it was, in case it was a spider – ugh! A few minutes later, the same thing happened to me again, this time hitting me on the head. It was obviously someone messing around.

I should have known. It was that stupid little boy, throwing M&Ms at me and then ducking down when I looked around to see who it was. I wished he would aim them at my hands – I was hungry! I told his mum and in true Indian style, she smacked him round the head and then took the packet away from him.

It was becoming lighter and the cloud formations were becoming more visible. I was no sniffer dog but I could smell the food being warmed up. It was no longer time for me to sleep.

Eating took all of three minutes. That was because I could only eat the potato curry and the piece of naan bread that was the size of a Maryland cookie. The remaining food consisted of a few grains of rice with chicken soup. Something that I would not eat even if my life depended upon it. I should have opted for the vegetarian meal. While Ally filled her face with all the food that was on her plate and half of mine, I was indulging in a large bag of salt and vinegar crisps that I had bought in the duty-free shop and sipping on my tea.

As I lay back on my seat I happened to come across the few M&Ms that the little shit had thrown at me. I left them on the side so I could return the favour when his mother was asleep. The food had obviously given people the energy that they were lacking. Further up the aisle, there was a game of musical chairs going on. Kids were racing up and down to swap places with each other. Their mother had no chance of sitting them down on their own seats. She was shouting at them but when do children ever listen, especially when they are in a little group of their own? All the fun ended when an old bag, I mean a woman, went and snitched on them. The mother had given up trying to control the four kids who looked similar in age, but as soon as the air stewardess came along they automatically returned to their seats and sat there colouring with crayons that she had cleverly supplied to keep them quiet.

In a confined environment such as an aircraft, there are not many things that people can do. They tend to have a nap as soon as they get on the plane, they wake up in time for the food and then go back to sleep again. Well, this group was no different. I attempted to do a crossword. I managed to answer two clues out of sixty, then I needed a helping hand from the pages at the back of the book. I thought now was a good time to test my throwing ability. So I threw the first little pea-sized chocolate M&M. It hit the window and landed on a lady's lap. Luckily she was sleeping, and if she was dreaming about chocolate her dream may have come true!

I tried for the second time but missed again. I fully understand why I was not allowed to throw a javelin for our sports day competition at school. I probably would have killed someone. Admittedly, I was incapable of aiming at a target so I persuaded Ally to have a go with the M&Ms. She got it in one, and the sweet hit the boy on the top of his arm. Both of us showed our guiltiness by laughing and looking over to see the little horror's reaction. He turned around and knew it was us.

The next thing we knew, he woke his mother up. He began to rub his left eye with his hand and said that we had thrown an M&M over and it had hit his eye. The conniving little so-and-so was about to get his mother on us. After taking a look at his eye, she rubbed it and asked him who threw it. Ally continued reading and I carried on filling the answers in the crossword. The mother was gaunt-looking with big brown eyes. Her skinny arms were covered with marks that had been left from measles or chicken pox. We did not look over but I could see her staring at us from the corner of my eye. I don't think she had the guts to accuse us of something she had not seen us do. However, we sniggered when we heard the mother telling her son off in Hindi.

13

I'm A Celebrity! . . . Get Me In There!

The flight had been eventful but it was now coming to an end: we had arrived at Mumbai. Another flight had landed at the same time, so it was like trying to squirm our way through the Notting Hill Carnival, not forgetting to lug our jam-packed suitcases along with us. We felt completely at home with our unwashed, sweaty look. Then we experienced what I thought was our first street robbery. An Indian teenage boy with the body-frame of an anorexic wearing ripped shorts, no top and barefoot, was running towards us. He took our suitcases and started casually walking in front of us.

Ally was gob-smacked. She was standing there in despair while I dashed ahead and finally grappled them off him. He had the audacity to ask us for a small financial reward for his so-called service. We ignored him but he kept following us around and mumbling a few words in Hindi, no doubt demanding his money. We were not the only ones being hounded by these con-artists who try to rip off foreigners: other people were experiencing the same thing. I was dead embarrassed and felt obliged to give him a few rupees just to leave us alone. After all I did have 40,000 rupees in exchange for £500.

There was supposed to be a car waiting for us outside the airport to take us to our hotel. The sun was blazing and the only water in sight was that which was dripping off people's skin. Sitting near the doors that led out to the streets was a woman in a faded green sari carrying her unclothed baby who was crying at the top of its voice. She looked directly at us and out of sympathy Ally gave her a rupee. She refused the money and pointed at my blimmin' boots, a pair that I was happy to take off but definitely not so I could give them to her. You would think she would be grateful for what she received - obviously not. We put the money in her little begging pot and walked into the streets of India. The smell was outrageous; the pavements were covered with rotting fruit and vegetables that had been trodden on by passing pedestrians. This attracted flies and hungry abandoned dogs, making me feel a little sick.

The roads were packed with cyclists, the ever so tiny black three-wheeler rickshaws and the taxicabs that were beeping at one another. The rules of the road were that there were no rules! You had to dodge the other road-users to get to your ultimate destination, having to deal with all the numerous obstacles that got in the way. There was no road safety system in force like in England. Oh God. It was all a bit much to take on board, especially for us first-time visitors. People were running around, carrying baggage, selling useless items and we were getting unwanted attention. We were being treated like celebrities!

The driver was holding up a piece of cardboard with the name Alisha Desai on it. We got into the car and the designated driver took us to our hotel. The road was bumpy and the driver was a nutter. As he approached a roundabout, he manoeuvred the car in such a way that the back door was flung open and Ally nearly fell out. She reached out to grab the handle and pull it towards us. Oblivious to this, the chauffeur carried on driving in the same maniacal way. After a death-defying fifteen-minute ride, we were standing next to our suitcases outside the Royal Raj Hotel with great relief. The building looked beautiful. It was made from fine marble, and the two massive pillars either side of the entrance gave it the appearance of a Greek building. I could see that the twelve stairs were going to be an ordeal to climb. Yet before we could look at each other and start groaning, a porter appeared, hefted our bags and sprang up the stairs two at a time. Our bags got to the top before we did! The doors opened automatically and instantly we could feel a breath of fresh air. In this case, it was better known as air conditioning. Bliss!

The hotel had a bar, an indoor and outdoor swimming pool, a leisure room and a gym. These were the first things that caught my attention while skimming the placard on the wall. The receptionist was overly nice and falsely enthusiastic, her American accent eliminating the authenticity of it all. We entered our boudoir via the card system and immediately explored it. It was an en-suite with a mini-Jacuzzi. Yippee! The room also had a balcony overlooking the town although it was not a very scenic view. I was tired – I think jet lag was kicking in – so I went to have a nap. Meanwhile Ally, 'the intrepid Indian bush trekker', went to explore the hotel and the various facilities that were available to us. Apparently, this place was a hot-spot for celebs. They were probably game-show hosts or local soap stars that we had never heard of, so there was no need for me to give my autograph book to Ally because she would not recognise them anyway.

We had dinner at the restaurant and spent the rest of the evening in the outdoor pool talking about what the holiday entailed. One of the free excursions included in this holiday package was a visit to the Bollywood film studios; it sounded quite exciting to see how a film was made. At nine o'clock the following day, a coach was going to pick us up outside our hotel, along with a few other people who were also staying there, and who had booked this tour as part of their holiday.

At five o'clock in the morning the local traders were already up and working hard to make a living. We closed our eyes against their clatter and calls and awoke hours later, just in time to get ready and run downstairs to the bus. If I had told Auntie Mira about this visit, she would have insisted that I obtain every C-list celebrity's autograph so she could show them off to her Bollywood-movie-loving friends. However, my mother had already beat her to this request. Huh! This was going to be a bundle of laughs.

The studio tour turned out to be a huge tourist attraction, just like the *Coronation Street* or *Eastenders* tour you can take in England, or, of course, the true Hollywood tours. There were queues of people waiting at the entrance well before the opening time. It was actually a good day to visit the studios because there were scenes being filmed throughout the day. Thanks to our VIP passes, Ally and I were allowed to jump the queue and went straight in for a personal guided tour. The set was not at all how I had imagined it would be. The backdrop appeared to be so realistic yet close up, we could see all the tricks of the trade. Thanks again to our VIP passes, Ally and I were allowed to go on the set and have a snoop around and talk to various members of the crew who were arranging the stage props. They appeared to be stressed out and were rushing to add the finishing touches to make the scene look that little bit more realistic. The other tourists were watching from a distance, standing behind metal bars that helped cordon off the area where the filming was taking place.

A girl was standing around not doing much so I went to ask her a few questions.

'How long does one scene usually take to film?' I said.

'It depends on the actors and actresses. Sometimes it can take hours, other times it can take days,' she replied.

When she sat down to do her make-up and read through her script, I realised that she was playing the lead role in the film.

Her brown skin had been disguised by a pasty white foundation that put her in the same league as Michael Jackson. I did not understand why they did that. If, for whatever reason, these *filmi* stars were going to make themselves appear to have a paler skin colour, it should at least be consistent. There is no point in slapping a ton of a lighter-coloured powder on the face when the neck, hands and legs are left in full view in their natural colour.

I went to join Ally who was roaming around. Phew! The artificial lighting made the place really hot and stuffy. Every five minutes, I noticed, the actress would break out in a sweat and require a touch more powder. Poor thing!

We really wanted them to get on and do the promised dance scene so we could have a laugh. They were supposed to start filming at twelve but the 'hero' had not turned up yet. We were kept waiting for ages and even the director was showing his last levels of tolerance He was a plump, short man with grey hair.

The set consisted of an open trailer that was disguised as a small shop selling newspapers, plastic bangles and Indian sweets. The owner only had a few lines to say, but he was carrying out a dress rehearsal before the real thing. A screen had been placed behind him to give the impression that his shop was situated in a park. It was an amazing illusion. If I had not known any better, I'm sure I would have walked straight into the screen, thinking that it really was a park!

'I'm shit-bored,' Ally whispered in my ear. 'I really need a drink, how much longer are they going to keep us hanging around?'

This was becoming exceedingly tedious. Everyone was waiting for this one shoot to take place. To pass time, the guide gave us a quick tour around the outside of the studio, but it was not very interesting. The sun was burning my skin - it was hot enough to fry an egg on it and I had forgotten to put sun cream on. Why were we waiting around for this plonker to turn up? Was he having a diva strop? The whole Bollywood boom had been hyped up so much, yet it turned out to be a huge disappointment. As for the films, they had a long way to go to reach Hollywood standards. Nevertheless, the Bollywood industry was becoming more and more successful. Considering that their budgets were nowhere near those available to the American movie producers, Bollywood was doing very well for itself, thank you.

We had been around the set nearly four times, having mini-conversations with the people who were taking part as extras in that scene. Small talk was hard work; they could more or less understand what we were saying because we used sentences that were constructed using the most basic words in Hindi but as they spoke very quickly we usually ended up only catching one or two words from each sentence and could only respond with a smile and an agreeing nod.

Only the superstars were important enough to be allocated an electric fan to cool them. The rest of us had to suffer the painful heat which was making us lethargic and irritable. The public was agitated and although many of the foreigners were happy to wait, some were demanding a full refund. A large Indian family of three adults, a couple of teenagers and a few kids who were visiting from Britain were arguing about whether to stay or go. The parents said that everyone should stay to see the film shoot, just to get their money's worth.

Indians are always late for everything. So for future reference if any of you are planning any surprise parties, make sure you tell them that it starts at least an hour earlier than it does. Maybe it is a cultural or genetic thing but that extra hour was obviously only relevant to the Indians living in the UK. From today's episode I could only conclude that the people residing in India turn up the 'delay' notch a couple of hours. I cannot speak for all, but let me tell you it is very common at Indian weddings for not only the bride to be a 'respectable' hour or two late, but also for the guests to arrive in dribs and drabs usually two hours after the commencement of the ceremony, but a minimum of half an hour before the buffet lunch, so as not to make it too obvious as to why they have turned up at all.

When I asked the tour guide what time the actor was going to arrive, she shrugged her shoulders as if to say that it could take a couple of hours, or he might not even turn up at all. Had the guy not heard of ringing into work to tell them that he wouldn't be coming in? It was all a shambles and a waste of time. I poked Ally hard in the ribs. 'Look, I don't know about you, but no way am I gonna wait around for some egotistic lazy-arse shit that I've not even heard of, to stroll in at whatever time pleases him just to say a few lines and then go home again.' I grinned at her. 'If we were waiting for Brad Pitt, then it would be a totally different story.'

'Let's call a cab and go back to the hotel' she said, as she lit up one of our duty-frees, only to be told sternly by our tour guide to put it out as she pointed at the big no smoking sign.

I sympathised with the fans and tourists who had paid to see the scene being filmed. Unlike the hardcore admirers who were willing to wait as long as it took, we decided to leave and go back to the hotel to relax and prepare for a night out on the town. Look, I don't want to sound ungrateful. If we had not been fortunate enough to be invited to attend the movie awards ceremony, then the visit to the Bollywood studios would have been much appreciated.

As the driver took us back to the hotel, he was chewing on betel nut (paan) - a type of tobacco that makes your teeth and the inside of your mouth and tongue go a reddish-orange colour. I found it really revolting, and felt that men who chewed it must be dirty. Don't ask me why, I just did. Subconsciously, this reaction must come from the stereotypical betel-chewing role that the baddies play in Bollywood movies. Of course, in India that would mean the majority of the male population! I think the taxi driver's teeth were rotten because of this disgusting habit. The problem is not that people chew the addictive plant extracts, but more so the process they use to get rid of the extra saliva that is being produced...by spitting! Urghhh!

I had seen people do it enough times back home when we made the odd shopping trip to Wembley or Southall, areas of north-west London heavily populated by Asians. They were not even discreet about where they spat. Just beside where they walked was good enough for them. They were oblivious to how offensive their behaviour might appear to others. Oh well, I'm no angel and have plenty of addictions of my own, like hot men and ice-cold G&T, but that spitting business will never get my vote.

Most of the cars, I noticed, looked exactly the same. The cabs were yellow and black with only the different registration plates to distinguish them from each other. When our driver stopped at the traffic lights, I noticed that we were parallel to another white car and I nudged Ally to take a look. It was a 'cartoon car', one I had never seen before. The rectangular roof, two elongated edges at the front and back, and the smooth, thin tyres made it look like a car from an animated film.

While waiting for the lights to change, our driver rolled down his window and spat out of it. Had the car been in motion, the wind could have blown that dirty gob of saliva back through the rear window, landing on me or Ally. As if that was not bad enough, in the hotel foyer that morning, I had overheard a traumatised guest telling another about her horrific journey.

The taxi driver who was bringing them back to the hotel had blown his snotty nose into his index finger and thumb and shook his hand vigorously out of the taxi window. I felt queasy at the thought of this, but could not stop myself eavesdropping. By the time I had heard how his snot flew straight through the rear window and landed on the passenger's cheek, I was retching. There was a lesson to be learned from this, I thought, feeling nauseated – always carry an extra packet of Kleenex tissues in my handbag!

I turned to look at Ally, whose face reflected my thoughts perfectly. There was a look of horror on it. I had not spoken aloud so why did she have that disgusted look on her face? Her reaction made sense when I noticed a blob of his reddish spit splattered against the 'cartoon car' that was parked next to us at the traffic lights.

In a rage, the other driver got out of his car and started swearing. He was wearing a stripy blue and white shirt that was undone, and his whitish fishnet vest had not done a very good job of covering up his hairy chest. His shirt was half-tucked into his dark-coloured trousers. Ally and I were sitting in the back, ducking our heads and laughing at him because he seemed to think that he was a member of the Mafia, ranting and raving about how he would remember our car registration number and get people to damage our car, property and family. Yet he had trouble remembering to zip up his own trousers. The rubber flip-flops on his feet were worn at the toes. He was walking around his car and heading towards us. Hey, were we in for an example of Indian road rage? Maybe we were about to witness some real, action-packed Bollywood fighting.

But with no apology from our driver, he quickly rolled up his window and we decided to lock our doors. The traffic-lights changed to green and the bus-driver behind us started beeping his horn. (There I was, thinking that London road-users were impatient!) So our driver took the opportunity of this slight distraction as a means of escaping; he slammed his foot down heavily on the accelerator and sped off. Mr Hairy Chest was left polluting the air with his foul language, looking like a complete moron.

Back at the hotel, we went straight into the lobby for a well-deserved drink. India was a culture shock, far from what we had expected. We only ever drank alcohol and smoked fags in our hotel (apart from that one occasion when Ally was so bored that she lit one up at the Bollywood studios) because people had strong beliefs about what girls should and shouldn't do. After all, we didn't want to create a bad image. However, if that's what it took to get through this experience with our sanity still intact – then so be it!

14
Paradise

Evening had approached, yet outside it looked as though it was still midday. Ally and I sat at the bar, beginning to relax and chill out as we waited for our new friends that we had met earlier on in the day. Natasha and Jasmine had travelled to India from Queensland, Australia. They had three days left before they made their way up north to New Delhi and then down south to the popular resort of Goa. They had taken a year out to travel the world. Both had been friends from a young age and were born into families where they used money like we would use water.

Natasha was a calorie-control freak. She was allergic to nuts and not very adventurous when it came to trying new dishes and drinks. The only reason she was mingling with us was because we were staying in the same hotel and therefore she assumed we were socialites too. Her snobby attitude gave us the impression that she thought she was better than everyone. I didn't mention to her that we had won the trip to India and thought I would add a splash of colour to my life by telling her that I was an aspiring actress. Why? I didn't want to tell them that I was unemployed, and therefore the next best thing that came into my head, with the movie awards in mind, was being an actress. Natasha was very interested to hear more...so I carried on, and in fact got carried right away.

Jasmine was submissive and took everything at 'face value'. She was in Natasha's shadow, but was very down to earth and definitely not a name-dropper. The pair found it difficult to adapt to the environment outside our hotel because it was a case of the material world versus the real world. The bar was empty and the barman was reading the paper, every so often glancing over in our direction with a cheeky smile.

The more we got to know the girls, the less we found we had in common. There was a culture clash between our social classes. Working-class bitches (us) versus upper-class super-bitches (them)! We flagged down a taxi and went into the town. Natasha wanted to pay an extortionate entry fee to go to Club Diva, a club renowned for celebrity spotting. Not because she had heard of them, because she hadn't - it was the production crew filming there for a local TV series that enticed her. Jasmine knew her opinion would make very little difference to Natasha's decision, so she agreed. Ally and I left them to it, simply because we could not afford it. My excuse, of course, was not that we had no money, but that I was tired of being in front of the camera and wanted to get away from it all. I could sense Ally sniggering behind me as I said this.

We went our separate ways and Ally and I decided to go to Club Paradise instead. The exterior looked shabby and the entrance fee was minimal. The security guard standing near the door was short and podgy – not really much of a threat, but it was the top half of him that could have made you run a mile. His shoulder-length greasy hair was left untied and his mean 'don't mess with me look' reflected the impression he wanted to give out. A shiny gold tooth could be seen every time he asked someone for an identity card. He was obviously no athlete, but his face was formidable enough to deter anyone from misbehaving.

We went in and for some reason attracted everybody's attention. Could it have been because we were wearing mini-skirts and halter-neck tops that made us stand out like sore thumbs? The other girls were dressed like they were going to school on a non-uniform day, wearing pleated knee-length A-line skirts and frilly loose tops, and the boys were revoltingly pervy. When we went to the bar and waited to be served, I only recognised a few of the spirits that were on offer and chose to drink them even though they were my least favourite ones, sticking to well-known brands such as Jack Daniel's.

Along came Mr Try-His-Luck, who totally invaded my personal space, by standing two inches away from me. This was definitely not a good start. All I wanted to do was hold my breath while he tried chatting us up with his broken English. Some XXX mints would have solved his halitosis within seconds. I was unable to tell whether his friends were laughing at him while they watched the dunce make a fool of himself, or at me, as I attempted to discreetly exhale the gasp of air that I took when I kept looking away every ten seconds.

The biggest cringe factor was his Bollywood-style outfit: he wore tight white jeans with a black T-shirt that appeared to be two sizes too small. I noticed his 'booster' black Cuban-heel boots that gave him those important extra couple of inches in height. We ignored him completely and waited for him to go back to his friends. Trying ever so hard to catch our attention, he lit up a fag, practically in front of our faces and offered one to us. I did want one but if I had taken it then I knew he would have latched on to us for the rest of the evening. He finally gave up and went back to the group of friends who were taking the piss out of him by mimicking his actions.

Club Paradise had a large floorspace and the dance floor was situated in the middle of the arena. Around the dance floor were tables, chairs, and a bar that was placed behind the seating area.

The name of the club came from the artificial palm trees and the half-blue and half-yellow painted walls. How uninspired! As Ally and I looked around the music became louder and the majority of the crowd started to strut their stuff on the dance floor. The tunes were ones that had already been heard by clubbers at least three or four years ago in the UK. It was going to be a night of listening to 'old skool' music. We were not drunk enough (well, Ally was getting there!) to embarrass ourselves by getting jiggy on the dance floor, so in desperation we started drinking neat shots of J.D.

It was all very civilised. There were no lager louts or ladettes barricading the club and the girls were dancing five inches away from their lovers, giggling every time they touched. The atmosphere was dull and it resembled a high-school prom. Even then, the high-school kids in the Western countries probably got up to more mischief than the people in this club did - and they were supposedly adults. So, to bump and grind, we figured that a change of venue was needed. As we left the club, I spotted a group of fit guys who also looked like tourists.

'Go on Al, speak to them,' I whispered. She shrugged her shoulders and before they went past us, I stopped them and smiled, asked them the time and then followed this with another question enquiring whether there were any good clubs in the area. Just as I expected, they were on their way to one themselves. A brief invite from one of the lads in the group was enough for us to follow them to a club just up the road from hellish Paradise. Ajay, Nick, Ash and Neil were out to enjoy their last night before flying home to London, where they all shared a flat in Holland Park.

There was one in particular to whom I had taken a fancy. Actually, two. Well all of them were good enough to be in *my* little black book. When it came to men, everything, it seemed was always against the odds and an uphill struggle. Knowing my luck, Ash was probably gay! Oh well, maybe there'd be a chance with one of the other three.

Suddenly, as if by magic, we were inside a club called Zamana and I had a drink in my hand. I was baffled - how had we got from one club to the other? I didn't remember walking there, but we must have. Not only that, I also had no recollection of waiting in the queue and entering the club. With all that chatting the alcohol must have built up and hit me all at once. I gave my drink to Ally who was looking rather green herself, and sensibly started drinking water.

From a piss-head's perspective, Zamana had a completely different atmosphere. This was the place where all the tourists were hiding; it was a trendy, modern set-up albeit small, and it had air-conditioning. Club Paradise didn't and if we had stayed there any longer, I probably would have dehydrated and fainted!

The girls who were already in Zamana were giving the 'evil eye' to any female newcomers. I stared round, gobsmacked, thinking I had died and gone to phatland! The boys were less sleazy here and better-looking...perfect. Mind you, perception of people and objects does change under the influence of alcohol. Once we girls have had one too many, we start to focus through our beer goggles; the mingers are in with a chance and all of a sudden they can take advantage of us vulnerable females.

I tried to hide the fact that I was totally off my face by acting sensible while I spoke to Ash in what I thought was my normal voice. But it transpired later that I nearly deafened him as the decibels increased with my excitement. Because of the active toxic chemicals whizzing around my bloodstream, I ended up asking him if he was gay! Only after it had been said, did I realise the implications of my words.

Oh my God! I couldn't believe I had said that to him. He, of course, was taken aback by my question, but being a good sport, he just grinned. Dead embarrassed by my motormouth, I then had to explain myself and tell him about the 'Deepak' situation. He was amused and also quite drunk, so there was still a small chance that he might not remember this conversation the next day. The good thing was that he *wasn't* gay. I think I would have given up and considered becoming a nun if he was! The best bit was that before I could say, 'Prove it,' he already had. Usually in my case, these encounters start off with a chat and the night ends with me threatening to obtain a restraining order to keep some weirdo away. For the first time, the evening started as per usual with a flirty chat, but it ended with the perfect kiss.

Ash was of athletic build with short black hair. His smile enhanced his defined jawline and revealed a set of straight, pearly-white teeth. This was going better than I expected. Now, what was the likelihood of finding myself a guy who was sexy, witty, intelligent and not gay? I think very slim, don't you? I definitely deserved a pat on the back. Ajay and Nick were on the dance floor with Ally, and Neil had disappeared on his own somewhere. The night came to an end with another snog and a promise to meet up when we were back in London.

The evening had been fantastic! However, in the early morning, Ally and I felt like bombs had detonated inside our heads. The previous night was an unfinished jigsaw puzzle. We lay in bed, the curtains drawn against the powerful sun, trying to fill in the gaps with our separate recollections of events. I did not want to get my hopes up, but a part of me was hoping that I would meet up with Ash when I got home. I adopted a blasé attitude about the whole thing, but I am sure that Ally was not fooled: she acknowledged my feelings. I could not stop thinking about him! We had so much in common...

Agreeing that we had had a fantastic night, Ally went to the phone booth to call Dylan and I dozed off until lunchtime. The afternoon was spent wisely. We made full use of the hotel's facilities by having a full body massage and a relaxing evening.

The movie awards ceremony was approaching. In the few days that we had left to ourselves, we went sight-seeing. We went to see Mumbai's most famous landmark, the Gateway of India. It was a colonial marker, a yellow arch of triumph that had been made redundant since the British departed India. It was educational – if you were in a history lesson – however we were hoping to go somewhere a little more exciting. Where better to go than Chowpatty beach! Great, I thought to myself, finally a chance to lie on the beach and sunbathe.

We got to the beach with our beach-bags and found that this was not a place where you could have a dip, nor was it one where you could wear a bikini and sunbathe. There was seaweed scattered on the sand and the smell of fish that had been caught early that morning to be sold on the market stalls was off-putting. We ended up walking along the shore, eating Kulfi, an Indian ice-cream made from milk and almond flavouring. In the daytime the beach was almost deserted, but it got much livelier in the evening. Balloon sellers and nut vendors had secured their places and beach entertainers were attracting crowds with their spectacular performances. It was like a mini-carnival.

On the last day, I had to go and visit my Aunt Hema who lived in one of the poorer parts of the city; my parents had asked me to give her something. The address was simply 'Flower Alley' – no number, nothing. Ally was hesitant about coming, but after enjoying watching me beg, she finally agreed to accompany me. The taxi driver dropped us off at the end of a road and directed us towards the flower alley on the left.

If the little alleyway had not been right under our noses, we would never have spotted it. It was overflowing with literally hundreds of carnations of all hues. The flowery scent was fresh, the path narrow and straight. The bushes there were heavily overgrown and attracted many insects. So many that I ran through the alleyway to avoid them, not realising in the distraction of it all that I did not know what house I was looking for. I asked a passer-by where Hema Malik lived. Luckily, I did not have far to go because, genius that I am, I had stopped right in front of her house.

We walked in and Auntie Hema welcomed us with a big hug. She was a replica of my mother – just a younger version. Her home consisted of two rooms. One was the kitchen and the other was divided into her bedroom and living room. Straight away she offered to make tea and before she gave us the chance to say no, she was in the kitchen making it. Just the thought of sweet, boiling hot milky tea in the scorching weather made me feel nauseous. It was the same old problem – how to say no without causing offence.

The house featured the bare necessities and although she was content with her lifestyle, I couldn't help but feel pity for my aunt. Uncle Rohan was an alcoholic. He would work all day and then spend the cash drinking and gambling throughout the night. His home was treated like a dosshouse and his wife was nothing to him but a woman who served his food on a plate. The floor had the odd ant wandering about, in addition to the odd hundred or so bees hovering around. I gave Auntie Hema the sari that my parents had sent over and Ally and I sat talking to her in our broken Hindi, some of which she probably did not understand because it was so bad.

After forcing herself to drink that tea through concern not to waste or leave behind a drop that a poor man would be grateful for, Ally needed to use the toilet to throw up. That was a good point - where the hell was it? We found out that the shower room and toilet was communal. It was situated outside in a hut that had been built from cement, right at the end of the one-way alley! I wondered how many people must have shat their pants while trying to make it all the way to the loo? Especially if they suffered from the runs! It was worse for the people who lived nearer to the beginning of the alleyway. I'm assuming that they would have to take torches with them when darkness approached.

We both needed to go but it was more urgent for Ally. She stood up, ready to go on her unforgettable pilgrimage to the toilet while I stayed behind. In hindsight it was actually a good thing. She went outside and took a couple of steps forward. Visibility was poor due to the flowers that were overcrowding the alley. Later, she told me that she finally made it to the hut and opened the door, only *to find no toilet*. Instead, there was a pear-shaped hole in the floor, next to a tap and a little beaker. I had figured from the snot incident that these people tended not to use tissues; however, it had not occurred to me that they did not use them to clean their bums either!

As Ally squatted to take a pee, she heard a disturbing noise. A mouse appeared from a hole in the wall. She screamed as she ran out, pulling up her pants. Battling her way back to the house, anyone would have thought she had been through a war. Almost in tears, she said there was a mouse in the toilet and then became angry and irrational at me for bringing her along. Fortunately, my aunt didn't understand.

'We have to get out of here, I'm sick of all this ethnic grot and I'm really starting to miss London!' she cried.

In the taxi, I was holding back my laughter because the state of her when she came back into the house was a one-off exclusive moment and I was very much in need of a Polaroid camera. Petals, broken twigs and a few leaves were incorporated into her hair and her face had become red from running in the heat. Poor thing!

I think she was really traumatised by the whole situation because she had very little to say on the way back to the hotel.

That evening, we rested and packed our suitcases for the following day's extremely early flight. It was goodbye to the

Royal Raj Hotel, Mumbai, and hello to the Samrad Hotel in the
capital city, New Delhi.

15
The Big Bash

The airport in New Delhi was busy, but there was no repetition of the kind of incidents we had experienced on arrival in Mumbai. Outside, the city was not as dirty as I had expected it to be; however there were plenty of trucks and lorries driving past emitting thick clouds of smog. But that was nothing new to us: after all, we lived in heavily polluted London!

Our driver picked us up and took us to the Samrad Hotel. The building was constructed of what appeared to be red, chalky rocks. I hoped it was not going to crumble while we were staying there! It was not as modern and well-kept as the Royal Raj but it was more of a traditional setting. Our bedroom was rather cramped and I was soon ungratefully complaining to Ally, saying that a four or five-star hotel in India was the equivalent of a B&B in Britain.

The Samrad was, in fact a three-star hotel, and perfectly adequate considering that it had cost us precisely nothing. If I had raised my voice only slightly, the receptionist would have heard me and I would have looked both ungrateful and stupid. The itinerary confirmed that we would have to stay in a three-star hotel in New Delhi. After giving it a few minutes' thought I came to the conclusion that the reason for this must be that the ones further up the scale had been reserved by the celebrities' agents well in advance.

Our room had twin beds, an en-suite shower cubicle and a fourteen-inch TV. Unfortunately there were no signs of a mini-bar, a Jacuzzi, or even a balcony, but we were far too busy preparing for the big night we had been so eagerly awaiting, so all my complaints vanished in a puff of ciggy smoke.

We were planning to spend the day seeing the sights and going to a shopping mall. But of course, sleep is always in our equation and sometimes can be the beginning, middle and end of the whole thing too - usually the result of drinking excessive amounts of alcohol the night before. It was time to take a quick nap to restore a sufficient amount of energy in order to survive the forthcoming event.

Our heads hit the pillow for what was intended to be a few minutes but which turned out to be a few minutes too many, as I found myself waking up later than expected. The one and only time you don't expect the alarm clock to let you down, the batteries take charge and terminate their existing lifespan.

It wasn't easy to undertake the enormous task of getting ready ten times faster than the usual four hours. It took me half of that time to squeeze into my dress. It was a red wine-colour, ankle-length, and I needed to wear four-and-a-half-inch heels to go with it. Nevertheless, I believed that if the celebs could do it, then so could I. The dress had a simple but elegant corset-style top, with embroidery and matching beads sewn onto it. The rest of the clingy material was left to flow of its own accord. The dress was pulled together with two strings that crossed over each other and tied at the lower end of my back. It really was a pain in the arse to wear but it did look absolutely beautiful.

With every layer of mascara that was applied, my lashes were growing. What was in this fabulous product? Amazed and continuing to make them as long as possible, I carried on. Soon, they were long enough to dip into a bucket of paint and use as a paintbrush to redecorate the walls. Applying lipstick had to be a 'car jobby', so that was the least of my problems. My next task was to do my nails with a quick-dry nail polish. Two coats of that and then sealed! This was fantastic. Pen correction fluid made my teeth white and so bright that I could use this as a device to cause temporary blindness if for any reason I had to get away. Wow! At last I was ready to go and felt pretty pleased with myself. I sat in the car and after several layers of lipstick, my lips were full-figured and I looked like a mini-version of Jordan. I looked absolutely stunning! There was something dreamlike about it all.

'Miss Nayak, Miss Nayak . . . How does it feel? Miss Nayak, Congratulations! Miss Nayak, what's it like to host an event as big as … Nina Nayak, when's the release of your next film?' The journalists and paparazzi were shouting over each other as soon as I got out of the car and walked on the famous red carpet. Like a true star, I stood and waved for the cameras before going in. The doors were magnificent; the events crew had replicated the *Stars in Their Eyes* set, with an artificial smoky effect occurring every time they were opened, leaving the public and journalists feeling more curious than ever.

Onstage, I was hosting the show. Yes, I know it sounds unbelievable, but the chairman of the awards ceremony asked me to use my outspoken nature to stir things up.

At first I declined. I wanted to be friends with the A-list celebrities, not bitch about them in front of their faces. But Ally said that I should consider doing it. 'If you can't join them…beat them!' she urged, so that's exactly what I was planning to do.

Oh no! I was appalling myself by saying the most horrible things to some of my favourite stars, but it was beyond my control. I was a mere puppet being manipulated by the puppetmaster.

'Now, the nominations for best female singer/actress: Beyoncé Knowles as a thunder-thigh, um...I mean a smooth spy in *Austin Powers*...J-Lo as an arsy cop featuring in *Out of Sight*...something her bum has trouble doing'. Britney Spears, I said, had the lead role in *Cross-eyed* – oops, I meant *Crossroads*, and last but not least, Mariah Carey sparkled things up by starring in *Glitter*, based on her own life of litter.

Although the four of them are not the best of friends, at that point they joined forces to come and kill me. It was just the right moment to get a grip and wake up. The dream was so vivid, I really thought I was actually there. I shook my head groggily. Where's the dream analysis book when you really need it?

'Ally, wake up!' I looked at the clock and there was still plenty of time for everything. I poked Ally until she opened her eyes, then I told her about my bizarre dream. She thought it was a bad sign, but stressed that nothing could possibly go wrong, because the company had organised everything. All we had to do was sit in the limousine and be there on time. Even our hair and make-up were being done for us courtesy of *Fashion* magazine so we had nothing to worry about.

We spent the rest of the day dripping sweat and going to see an historical fort. Local people stared at us as we walked past. Even though we shared the same religion and traditions, we were still treated like foreigners. Maybe it was because I kept rubbing mosquito repellent into my skin while walking along the streets. I could visualise myself covered in red blotches on the day of the movie awards, so I was taking no chances.

We paused near a bus stop, where a man was selling fresh ice-cold juices. The cups were so small I had four refills and that *still* had not quenched my thirst. I was too embarrassed to ask for another one because the third time I asked him to refill my cup, he looked at me weirdly. The gorgeous red evening dress I had worn in my dream sadly did not exist in real life, so we decided to take a trip to the shopping mall to buy ourselves a special outfit. Ally wanted to experience an Indian bus ride while I opted for the quick and efficient way around town - a cab. Arguing over what method of transport to choose and knowing that there was a taxi passing by more often than a bus, we agreed to take whatever came first.

Luck was on Ally's side, as a bus was just approaching. The windows were dusty and the vehicle appeared to have been on some sort of safari before it stopped to pick us up. The passengers were already squashed in tight. There was no way we would be able to get on. I couldn't understand why Ally could possibly want to go on that hellish bus when it looked as though it was about to fall apart. I think she still had not got over the 'toilet situation' and wanted to punish me. I was hoping it would go straight past us, but the driver stopped and opened the door. I heard him shout to the others to move back and we squeezed inside. A woman was so close to me, I could smell the coconut oil in her hair - at least it wasn't body odour, or something worse, as experienced on the dear old London underground. The bus was packed full with so many Indians, it felt a bit like a lorry loaded with illegal immigrants trying not to miss the transfer to another country.

Ally was blocking the door with her Mary Poppins bag and I was praying that she would not find space to move it over, so we could get off this stupid bus and opt for a cab. Indeed my prayer came true. At the next stop we got off the funny-smelling bus and flagged a cab instead. All thanks to her big-arse bag!

The shopping mall was smart with the majority of stores selling Indian suits and dresses. There was also an outdoor market with various types of stalls. People from nearby villages were selling unique handmade beaded jewellery, paintings, clothes and other pretty souvenirs. The stores were busy selling designer outfits and footwear too.

We entered an independent store that specialised in evening wear. The assistant was of no help; she needed to take a fashion course if she was planning to share *her* advice. I ended up buying a long black satin halter-neck dress with a plunging neckline and a slit on one side. Ally's dress was royal blue with a ruffled top held up by two very thin straps. Again, the dress was long with a slit on the side. Next we went outdoors to find jewellery to match our dresses, and also to buy souvenirs for friends and family. We could have bought everything from the stores, but I thought it would be money better spent if we bought things from a poor person to help them earn a living.

As we walked through the market, men and women tried to charm us into buying their products. Just because we were foreigners, they automatically tripled their selling price, thinking that we would be stupid enough not to know any better. But we were Londoners, we'd been around the block and knew a thing or two ourselves. We knew the tricks of the trade. As soon as the buyers look uninterested, the seller instantly reduces the price of the item. I was no bargain-hunter but I was not going to pay triple the price just because I was a foreigner in that country. I couldn't believe I was being ripped off by another Indian. How terrible is that?

I was about to walk away from a certain stall in disgust when out of desperation the stall-owner came down to what seemed a more reasonable price. Oh my God, I was turning into my mum, who would haggle for everything she purchased. In Britain it is bad enough trying to barter in markets, let alone in retail stores. That's why I never go shopping with her. I guess it was fine to do it in India because that is a common feature of their trading.

By midday, the market was jam-packed with the local residents buying their daily fruit and veg. Before heading back to the hotel, we stopped off at a little café for something to eat.

The handwritten menu offered various dishes. I ordered a special biryani (rice with mixed vegetables). According to the waiter, it was a little spicier than the normal one. I was an Indian – I could handle hot food, I boasted.

The service was efficient and the café was clean. It was in need of modernisation but the posters and pictures of Bollywood stars did a good job of concealing the cracks in the wall. Along came the food and Ally and I dug in. As she tackled her naan and potato curry, I tucked into my biryani. Special? I'll say! After about two mouthfuls, I felt like I was breathing fire. The dish was so damn hot that my eyes watered and my nose ran. I felt so stupid after having boasted that I could handle my spicy food (well, I could back home), so out of pride I continued to eat a little more whilst gulping down pints of water. It was like chewing on red-hot chilli peppers dipped in Tabasco sauce.

Later that evening, we skipped dinner back at the Samrad Hotel. It would have been rude to stay in the city that invented the phrase 'Delhi belly' and not experience one. It must have been the food we ate earlier in the day! The night was spent dashing in and out of the loo while watching a Hindi film, trying to remember the actors and actresses just in case we saw them at the awards ceremony.

On the next day, Ally and I experienced one of the highlights of our holiday – and possibly of our lives – when we went to see the Taj Mahal. One of the Seven Wonders of the World, it was built in Agra by a Mogul emperor as a mausoleum for his wife and himself. It was fascinating to see the building's brilliant white exterior, made from a precious marble that had been beautifully carved. A photographer there kept pestering us to buy a photo that gave the illusion of us holding up the spire. He wouldn't stop hassling us and showing us photos of other people who had done it. I felt obliged to buy one just to shut him up. In the event, our families loved these photos so much that we were glad we had given in to him. That evening, back at the Samrad Hotel, we had a couple of beers in the bar, then embarked on the mega-task of preparing for the extravaganza.

'Do you think this will be as glamorous as Hollywood events?' Ally asked, as she applied her facemask. 'I don't think so, but we'll have to wait and see,' I answered, while I painted my nails. We wanted an early night so the following day would arrive faster.

And then it finally arrived. Hurray! The climax of our trip: the day of the movie awards. We were meeting Sarina (the stylist) at her salon in the afternoon; she was also the organiser of this annual event.

I woke up and the first things my eyes focused on were my nails. Oh bollocks! I had gone and fallen asleep with them only partly dried. They had printmarks all over them. I lay in bed feeling a tad anxious about the night ahead.

We were working against the clock. Once Ally and I had got out of bed and were dressed, we had to go to the salon to beautify ourselves. Sarina did a brilliant job with our hair and make-up. It took her all of twenty minutes to make us look like celebrities. It is funny what make-up artists are capable of creating. Thanks to them, famous people always have the opportunity to shine radiantly in public, even if they are naturally butt-ugly!

By half past five, Ally and I were sitting nervously in the hotel foyer, waiting for the car to pick us up at six on the dot. Sarina had told us to arrive a little earlier to avoid the rush-hour traffic and to sit in a bar that was two minutes away from the hall of fame. The driver was pottering along at about ten miles per hour, so we might as well have been stuck in the rush-hour traffic – at least that was a more acceptable excuse for being late. Maybe he was asphyxiated by the combined fumes of my Armani perfume and Ally's Chanel fragrance.

In the car I made up three rules that we had to adhere to during the evening, to spice things up a little. After all, we weren't going to know anyone there and none of the people attending were ever going to see us again. So why not make the most of the night? The rules were:

    – To lie through our teeth about who we were, our occupations, status and anything else in that regard.

    – Enjoy ourselves, flirt, and find out who the important people were.

    – Make contacts – they might be useful in the years to come.

After hearing the rules, Ally agreed enthusiastically. Simple enough, weren't they? Yet it was becoming harder to remember them after several alcoholic beverages had made it down my throat. We planned to get tipsy before we got to the ceremony, since this would soften the snobby atmosphere that we were about to enter. The whole prospect was intimidating to say the least, and we had not even arrived yet.

In the bar we sat at the counter and drank like there was no tomorrow. Bar B was nothing special. It had comfortable leather seats, which had already been taken by a group of fans waiting to see their favourite stars and celebrities. Through the window, we could see that journalists had arrived, along with the photographers, who had chosen good spots and were setting up their equipment. A white van was parked in front of the entrance; it looked like a film vehicle for one of the cable channels. A barrier had been erected on the street parallel to the entrance of the Hari Om Music Hall for the public to stand behind it and watch. Some fans had already started queuing, holding up banners and posters. The more we psyched ourselves up, the more drink we needed. My feet were already starting to kill me in those stupid sandals. However, the pain was the least of my worries. I needed to concentrate on keeping an equal balance on each foot so that I didn't buckle.

The good old Tennessee sourmash whiskey was starting to work its magic and all of a sudden I had plenty to say (I was practising my new posh English accent). Ally gulped down her drink and suggested that we get going. For some reason, she was under the impression that I had already drunk far too much. To be honest, I think she was right.

As soon as we could see people making their way to the entrance, we decided it was time for us to walk down the famous red carpet. The atmosphere was unimaginable: journalists were hollering questions, hoping that some celebrity would stop to answer them; the public (now in their hundreds) were shouting and sticking their hands out for just one touch or an autograph. Dozens of people were taking photos and some were filming the event using camcorders as big as old style ghetto-blasters. It made us feel self-conscious. Right – here goes! The screams got louder as we came nearer. Little did we know that we had, in fact, picked the worst moment to take this attention-seeking stroll past the media.

All of a sudden the Indian public were booing and hissing at a celebrity whom they loved to hate. Sunita Sharma played the role of a nasty character, Pinky Herami, in one of India's most popular soaps called *Meri Kismet* (My Fate) that was watched by millions. These unsophisticated viewers were unable to understand that she was only *acting* in that soap – and even went so far as calling her by the character's name instead of her own. Being the two muppets that we were, Ally and I minced along directly behind her – and even though the comments were not aimed at us, it felt like we were getting dissed as well. This star made it worse for herself as she walked straight ahead, looking down: she did not wave, smile or even look up for the cameramen.

Ally and I took our time as we walked down the aisle; we paused and smiled, just like the rest of the film stars, for the photographers to get quick snapshots. I was trying not to blow my cover by showing that I was overwhelmed by being in the limelight.

If you want to be treated like a celebrity, you have to act like one. That five-second walk felt like my fifteen minutes of fame. It was fantastic and I can totally understand how people get addicted to the attention-seeking lifestyle. Ally and I loved every minute of it.

As we went in my legs were shaking from all the commotion. It was a considerable challenge pretending to be a confident actress and smiling for the cameras while walking in painful sandals that might give way at any moment. But we had walked the walk, and now we needed to talk the talk. Next we had to pass along a narrow corridor with lots of security guards conducting thorough searches; the walk was so long that the alcohol was starting to wear off.

Inside the hall, the layout was similar to that of an opera house. Round tables were scattered across the floor, each seating eight guests. We were placed at a table in the corner, at a short distance from the stage. I lie: our table was so far from the stage, we would have needed binoculars to see the host. The lighting was kept to a minimum; it was so dim that there was more chance of finding Wally (remember those hilarious *Where's Wally* books?) than of pinpointing our table.

The list of people who were supposed to be attending this event included many actors and actresses whom I had never heard of, along with directors, producers and scriptwriters. However, even I recognised Salma Hayek sitting further up front, and Meera Syal was there too. Ally and I were thrilled, as we thought she was great. I also recognised a few of the Indian film stars who strolled in. For instance, the guy who played the lead role in the Hindi film that we were watching the night before at the hotel had also turned up. But on the whole it was too dark to be a star-spotter and my attention was soon diverted to the champagne that was being served by the waiters. Ally and I took full advantage of the 'on the house' offerings.

Sipping at our glasses of champers we looked round and waited for the rest of the guests at our table to turn up. The whole thing was nowhere near as disconcerting as I had expected it to be, mainly because we were shoved into the corner where no one could see us. I'm sure the alcohol played its part too, in calming our nerves.

The lengthy process of getting everyone seated was becoming dreary for those of us who had arrived early. Finally, everyone was seated and we met the four people who had joined us. Two had not turned up. One man had brought his wife along and the other two were friends. At first we all ignored each other, but then I remembered rule number three. So I introduced myself, and the trend caught on.

The two men were a director and a scriptwriter, and of course the two women were actresses. I was astonished that I was actually sitting next to James McMillan. He had directed the box-office hit *Cover up*. So why the hell was he seated over here with non-entities like us? I later found out that he could not stay the whole evening, so he had been seated here to enable a quick exit. Great, so this table was reserved for people who were in two minds about turning up or for those who were sneaking off early.

Finally, the show started. We applauded all the nominations and then the winners too. As long as the tray of glasses with ice-cold champagne was passing by, I was happy. However, the novelty was starting to wear off. It was like a graduation ceremony. At first everybody is delighted, but then it reaches a point where only the person graduating is excited. For the rest of those present, it becomes a struggle to stay awake. James McMillan had left halfway through and all the people sitting at our table had been drinking for hours. I was in desperate need of the toilet, so I made my way there by going round the tables, discreetly holding on to the chairs to stop myself from toppling over. I wasn't drunk - it was my sandals!

The walls in the powder room were covered with mirrors from ceiling to floor. I was adding a bit of colour to my lips when I heard the toilet flush and a girl emerged from a cubicle. I recognised her from a Hindi film she had starred in and which I had watched with my aunt. I smiled and she offered a false smile in return.

'Hi, I'm Nina.'

'Hi, I'm Reshma.' She stood before the mirror, applying some extra powder to her nose.

'Your recent movie was a big hit in Britain –.' I began, but before I could finished my sentence, she rudely interrupted with: 'Does it look like I care?' while putting her powder compact back in her bag.

Astonished and hurt by her unfriendly attitude, I said:

'You didn't let me finish. You weren't all that good. In fact, you could barely act. It was your co-star who made the movie a success.'

She was not expecting this shocking response, and to be honest, neither was I. With a look of disgust, but nothing to say, the bitch walked out to join her colleagues. With her rotten attitude that had passed its sell-by date by months, there was absolutely no way I was about to tell her that several sheets of bog roll were stuck to her shoe and trailing along behind her.

The spotlights were so bright in the toilets that my eyes found it difficult to re-adjust to the dim lighting in the main arena. Suffering from temporary blindness, I headed back to Ally before she sent out a search party.

I sat down, noting that I must have just missed Ally on my way over. I looked at my watch and still attempting to maintain my posh British accent, asked what time this event was going to end. The guy sitting next to me answered my question and said, 'I think you're sitting at the wrong table.' I looked around and he was right, I recognised no one. They were busy watching the nominations, so it was not quite one of those 'curl up and die' moments.

I apologised and as I stood up, the man introduced himself as Mr Bachu Zooka. What a funny name, I thought to myself. Bazooka, bazaar, bizarre, buzzzz! The words just would not stop going round in my head! Finding it difficult to concentrate and not quite remembering his name, I was trying to ignore those damn words that were playing on my mind. It was supposed to have been a silent conversation I was having in my head. I did not realise that I had said, 'Stop it!' loudly enough for the man to hear.

'Sorry – what was that?' he said.

'Oh, I'm Nina,' I stated boldly, grasping his hand and shaking it firmly.

I finally had the opportunity to display my acting skills by saying that I was a British actress because Mr Bazooka – I mean Mr Zooka – had the decency to ask. He was intrigued and I was obviously impressing him with my imaginary career. A director of Bollywood movies, he was apparently in the middle of making a new one which was going to be released the following year in the UK. He was fascinated by my British accent and said he could offer me a cameo role. A brief synopsis of the film suggested that it was about the way in which Eastern culture was influencing Western culture. Mr Bachu Zooka wanted British actors and actresses to play characters living in the Western world and Bollywood stars to play the opposing characters in order to make the film as realistic as possible.

I played along because I wasn't quite sure whether he was being genuine or whether I was being stupidly gullible, so I said that I would discuss it with my agent, pointing at Ally, who was watching the nominations and looking very bored. Oh my God, what the hell was I doing? He handed over his business card and asked me to come by his office the next morning. Of course, the incentive was money. Cameo roles aren't voluntary you know! He asked for my card. I had the cheek to say that actresses in demand never have any business cards left towards the end of the evening, and stood up to go back to my table.

It was the alcohol that had caused this mess. Now the roles were reversed: he was the gullible one and I was gooooooood! A champagne glass was taken from the tray, drunk in celebration and then replaced by another full one before I sat down. Disaster followed. My bum hit the chair and the chair hit the floor. As I sat down, the front chair-leg had collapsed, making the rest of the chair topple over. Some dickhead from a neighbouring table had swapped his broken one with mine. Ally started laughing and one of the other guys on our table helped me back up. Instead of standing around, waiting aimlessly for my replacement chair, I headed for the toilets again, this time with Ally. I was too drunk to care about falling over, figuring that no one would have seen me because it was too dark.

I wanted to tell her about Mr Bazooka; she was pleased for me, but even more thrilled about being my agent. I was trying to talk myself out of it, but she was using all her powers of persuasion to talk me *into* it. By that stage, we were both completely rat-arsed and were talking utter shite. The only reason I believed I had had that conversation with Mr Bazooka was because his business card was in my handbag.

It had turned out to be an interesting night, all right. The party afterwards was probably brilliant. Unfortunately, we weren't invited to it, but we had other plans anyway. Sleep! Towards the end of the evening, my memory became very vague and to be honest I can't really remember how we got back to our hotel. But I woke up the next morning with a banging headache, lying on the floor beside my bed. I'm still not sure whether it was my hangover or whether I had fallen off the bed during the night!

I looked over at the other bed to see if Ally was okay but there was no sign of her. I shouted her name, but it came out more like a whisper. There was no answer. My heart was palpitating rapidly. I could not even remember coming home with her, so where the hell was she?

Weak and still pretty drunk, I tried to stand up to see if she had left me a note to say that she was going out, but she was a lazy slut: there was no way that she would have woken up that early. I was frightened that something might have happened to her. I checked in the bathroom: she was not there. There was a knock on the door...

My heart had frozen as I went to open the door. I was flattening my upright punk-rock hairstyle with my hands so that I would not scare the person off. Oh, there she was, the stupid cow, lying on the floor on the other side of the bed. She probably never made it on there in the first place.

I opened the door and it was the chambermaid, asking if we wanted our room cleaned. It was in too much of a state to let her clean it, and she would have had to run her trolley over Ally to even gain entry to the room, so I declined her offer. However, that meant we had to clean the damn room ourselves. A perfect hangover cure!

I emptied out my evening bag from the night before and seeing that business card with '2.30' written on it, it suddenly struck me that I had arranged to go and see Mr Zooka at his office this very afternoon. I couldn't remember what I had said to him, so I would have to be evasive when answering questions. Saying 'Yes' and 'No' without elaborating would have to suffice.

I tried to cure my hangover by going to have a nice long shower. Gradually, all the champagne, tobacco fumes and pretension of the night before were washed away and I began to feel better. Afterwards, I woke Ally and informed her of the meeting with Mr Zooka. In a state of confusion, she crawled into the bathroom to have a shower while I tidied up the messy room. She came out looking less green and sickly, thank God.

I phoned Room Service for a continental breakfast and some coffee. None of that Indian *chai*, thanks very much. I knew that neither of us was hungry, but we needed something to fortify ourselves before we got ready to go and blag our way into the scenic world of Bollywood acting. This really was diabolical!

16
A Bollywood Blag

After a fast ride in a taxi to Sualatra, an outlying suburb of New Delhi, we got out of the cab and headed towards a little cabin situated on what looked like farming land. Mr Bachu Zooka's workplace could easily have been mistaken for a foreman's temporary office on a building site. I was trying to tell Ally that I wouldn't be able to pull it off; it was the alcohol that had been doing all the talking. But she said that we could still blag it, so we knocked on the door.

'Come in,' said a deep voice. It was Bazooka himself. He beamed in a friendly fashion and I felt myself relax.

'Ah, I was hoping that you would come. Please take a seat.' He pointed at the chairs.

I introduced him to Alisha Desai – my agent – and she played her part with gusto. We were both surprised when he renewed his proposal and produced a contract. I had never really taken any of this seriously. Ally was already showing signs of being a novice. It was the amount he was prepared to pay for one scene that caught her off-guard. While she gibbered, her eyes glazing over again, I took the paper and had a quick overview.

My eyes focused on the payment. This stupid, I mean very nice, man was paying me 40,000 rupees for two scenes that were going to take approximately four hours to film. That amounted to just over £500 or more than £100 per hour. That sum was like winning the lottery for someone who scraped by on the dole.

Before signing, I read the scene, making sure it involved no singing or dancing; I also scanned the story-line to check that I was not appearing in a porno movie. For every good question asked, my 'agent' cancelled it out with a bad one. Trying to be a negotiator, she said that it was a cash deal or nothing. At which point I was going to smack her round the head. What the idiot failed to realise was that the majority of people and businesses in India dealt in cash anyway! That was such an 'Indian' thing to do, even back in London. Most of the older generation carry wads of cash in their pockets, 'just in case they make an impulse purchase'. What they don't realise is that the plastic cards allow them to do the same thing!

I informed Mr Zooka that I had only one day left before I headed back to London. I must have made quite a good impression at the awards ceremony because he changed his schedule to work around me. No one had ever done that before, and for the first time in my life I felt important and in demand. I was to play two different characters, a gangster's sister for one scene and then the manager of a club in London for another. He wanted someone with a genuine English accent, something Bollywood stars found difficult to attain.

All I had to do was deliver a few lines in my own voice. I had to be there at five in the morning the next day to do my scenes and get my money. At that point, I began to feel pangs of guilt. I felt really bad lying but I consoled myself by thinking that if I had not done it then someone else would have got the part, not forgetting that Mr Zooka would have had to conduct auditions for this tiny role, prolonging the process. Anyway, whatever happened to checking credentials? I might find it easier obtaining a job back home, I thought, if everybody hired you on trust.

Back at the hotel, I started practising my lines...but we were still very hung-over. We must have looked really rough when we went to see Mr Zooka. The two old bags needed an early night in with junk food for restoration purposes. We spent the evening lying on our beds watching TV and laughing at the poor acting. I was still thinking about what had happened earlier and I could not believe my luck! I was going to meet the leading characters in the film - how exciting was that? I made a mental note to take my autograph book with me.

The next morning we made our way to the Delhi film studios. The journey was strangely uneventful. Apart from a few bumps and dips in the road, there were no crazy drivers causing road rage. I think this was the first time we had used a taxi driver who actually had a driving licence - it was displayed on his dashboard. That partly explained the smooth trip. The other reason was that it was only a quarter to five in the morning! Now who in their right mind would be driving at that time? Apart from us.

The director was the only one who was wide-awake and chirpy at five o'clock in the morning. A scene was already being filmed and the next take was in preparation. I was briefly introduced to all the actors. Lo and behold, there she was – that cow I had met in the toilets at the awards ceremony. She was in the lead female role. This meant war!

'Hello, Reshma,' I said in a devious manner. She looked and smiled because the director was there.

'Oh, so you know each other?' he questioned.

'We had a run-in the other day,' I answered smoothly. I was sure that he did not understand what I was talking about and therefore just laughed it off. However, just one glimpse of her ruined my day and anger built up inside me. 'Always make the best of a bad situation,' my schoolteacher once told me. Good advice: I intended to follow it. I was going to make sure that Reshma suffered the repercussions of my wrath, seeing that she had caused it in the first place.

We prepared the set, I rehearsed my lines with Ally, and I was ready to act out the scene. Lights, camera, action!

'Look, you ain't going near my brother. He don't want no bitch from the valleys of North India or wherever you're from,' I said, as I played the character of Pooja (the sister of a high-profile gangster). If I had known that I would have to wear a bandanna, big fat black shades and a capped gold tooth, then I would have gone the whole way and worn a black eye-patch too. I tried to tell them that I was dressed more like a pirate than a gangster, but the stylist thought this image worked well. No wonder these 'Follywood' films can't be taken seriously. I looked a right prat. The good thing was that you could not even tell it was me! Thank God!

Reshma was playing the character of Neelam, a naïve village girl who was caught up in the criminal underworld. The scene consisted of a struggle between Neelam (Reshma), and Pooja (me). She was wearing a red sari blouse and a long, granny-smith-apple-green skirt of the sort that is usually worn by Indian women underneath their saris.

I grabbed her hands and shoved her to the floor . . . *Cut!* The director was amazed that it took only one take.

Now it was time for the nitty-gritty. 'Okay girls, you're doing well, carry on . . . ready? Lights, camera, action!'

Pooja (me) shoved Neelam (Reshma) on to the floor and tilted her head to the side by grabbing her hair. She was screaming in Hindi, 'Let me go, you stupid cow! I hate you!' *Cut.*

The director was fascinated by how well we worked together. He could not stop praising us, which would have been very flattering if we had been acting. But we weren't! I was going to teach her a well-deserved lesson.

It was great – I got to pull her hair and slap her. I cleverly made sure that it took a couple of takes because obviously I had not mastered the technique and needed the practice. She had to take all my abuse without being able to lay a single finger on me. Of course the gag helped because she could not tell the director that I was hitting her too hard until the scene was over. Wicked!

Being an actress was tiring. I was becoming very hot and paranoid that the mosquito bite on my chin would show up on screen. Reshma went to complain to Mr Zooka. I just hoped she was not going to hire a hit man to kill me before I went back home. Ally was standing by the side laughing her head off at the director's positive comments and at my actions.

The other scene was much shorter. All I had to do was deliver a few lines while answering the phone as a manager working in Britain, and *voilà!* All was completed. The director took us out for lunch in a café nearby to thank us for doing him a favour. I was praying that the film would get bad reviews so that none of my family or friends would go to see it. But would Ally be able to keep her gob shut? I doubted it.

Ally and I decided to wait until we were back in London to spend our windfall. We would have a little trip to the exclusive stores in Bond Street. That evening, our last in India, was humid and after packing, I dreamily lay in bed thinking about the twists and turns of this trip and the recent ups and downs of my life. Alas, this wonderful, surprising trip was over. I couldn't thank Ally enough for choosing me to share it with her. I turned to tell her this, but she was slumped under the bedclothes, fast asleep.

The next day, we were on our way home to London. Our lack of sleep was restored on the plane. I was awake in time for the food, but went back to sleep after eating it. The journey seemed much smoother this time than on the way there. Maybe it was because we were too tired to pay attention to any turbulence. There were no mischievous imps throwing sweets at passengers and everyone seemed to have taken a chill pill.

At Heathrow Airport, Ally's parents were waiting to pick us up. Her mum asked us twenty questions before we could even answer one. The sun had followed us back to the UK: amazingly, London had a blue sky with not a single cloud in sight. It was so nice not to come back from a warm country into a cold one.

Yet, everything felt peculiar. India had seemed so foreign at first, but we had gradually got used to its ways, and I felt a certain sense of loss. The 'Bollywood dream' had been left behind, along with the hustle and bustle, dodgy toilets, insects and the scorching sun, and now we were back among our London pubs, clubs, shops, and fast-track lives. We were happy to be home.

17
Life After Fame

Things returned to normal in no time at all. Before I knew it, I was back where I started, with no job, not much of a life and still no man. Ally enjoyed telling everyone how we ended up starring in a movie, and all about our adventurous trip. Things got a little out of hand, thanks to my mum who exaggerated things when telling the rest of our family. They kept asking me questions . . . not about *me* being in the film though – they were more interested in the other famous stars who were appearing in it, and curious to know what they were really like. Of course I told the truth. Reshma was unfriendly and nasty, but the rest of them were pleasant.

I had been in London for a few days before I received a call from Ash. The worst thing was that I couldn't really remember what he looked like. Although I had memories of him being attractive, I was hoping false images had not been implanted into my brain via the usual route - yes, I'm talking about alcohol. However, when we actually met up for a drink, my first impressions were happily confirmed. All the memories from that one evening came flooding back. Hours passed by, and our conversation was flowing like a river. I felt as if I had found my perfect match. It was hard to believe that we lived so near each other, and yet we had met in a different country. I started to make a long list of potential excuses just so I could go and see him.

Ash was a year older than me and worked in a large Japanese-owned company as a graphics designer. It was great! As long as his project was finished by the given deadline, he could pick and choose the days he went into work.

Things were finally starting to look up for me. I received an e-mail from Sarah Patterson, the editor of *Fashion* magazine, enquiring about our trip and asking if I would consider writing an article about our experiences. I got on to it straight away, seeing that the journey was still fresh in my mind. Ally and I summarised the trip, highlighting some good points and some negative ones. I sent it back to Sarah and took the opportunity to ask if there were any current vacancies. Two days later, I got a phone call from Sarah informing me that she had read my article and loved it. Would I carry on supplying them with other articles (the subjects to be discussed) on a freelance basis? The answer was: Yes please!

As for Ally, well, Dylan did propose to her. She accepted but the date is still to be confirmed. Considering that her folks haven't the faintest idea that she has an Australian boyfriend, let alone that she is engaged to him, she will have some major explaining to do. She has found herself a temporary job working in an advertising company and is saving up to go on holiday with Dylan to Australia to meet his parents for the first time. Scary!

I've come to the conclusion that my destiny doesn't involve a nine to five job. Nevertheless, nothing in this life is predictable. Things will always occur when they are least expected. I experienced my fifteen minutes of fame by playing the ultimate game of 'faking it' and blagging my way into the Bollywood industry as an actress. Who knows what the future holds? I might end up being the first female Asian Prime Minister (yeah right!) or maybe even a spy.

At this present moment in time, I am still dazed and confused but at least I am no longer sponging off the government, thanks to my job writing features for *Fashion* magazine, and my relationship has lasted longer than a week.

Two out of three is good enough for me! There's a big phat world out there, and although good girls *really* shouldn't... we almost always do.

BORN ON THE WRONG SIDE
Cec Thompson

300pp plus 16pp b/w photographs.
ISBN: 1-905147-17-1
RRP £11.99

From humble beginnings to sporting triumph and beyond, one of Rugby League's all-time greats tells his compelling story. An inspirational and candid autobiography of one of the first black men to represent the UK at Rugby League.

'It is what Cec Thompson has done with his life overall that is so moving . . . through effort, perseverance and a frankly astonishing all-pervasive desire to educate himself, he has earned the respect of not just the rugby league community but a much wider constituency' – *The Times*

THE HOUSE OF SUBADAR
Vijay Medtia

208pp
ISBN: 1-901969-27-4
RRP £11.99

The Subadar family lose their farm and way of life in the Punjab and make the harrowing 12-day journey to Bombay, convinced the streets will be paved with gold. The reality is harsher than they could have imagined as they exchange the drudgery and poverty of one slum for another. Success and happiness eventually come, but it is short-lived as others grow jealous of their wealth. This is an epic journey through the states and villages of India, offering beautiful descriptions and panoramic views of Punjab, Gujarat and Rajasthan.

'A remarkable début – a celebration of family and hope' – Sue Baker, *Publishing News*

BRIXTON ROCK
Alex Wheatle

270pp
ISBN: 1-901969-15-0
RRP £7.99

Winner of the London Writers Prize

In the days that preceded the Brixton Riots in 1986, author Alex Wheatle observed the tension building before it erupted into what is one of the most famous incidents of unrest in recent history. *Brixton Rock* is his story of a black teenager coping with life in 1980s Britain. He entertains us with colourful descriptions of South London street life as his tale unfolds, at once both comic and tragic.

'Sharp-edged and sardonically funny, *Brixton Rock* is Graham Greene for the hip-hop generation' – *Crime Time*

'A début which confirms its author a pro in prose' – *The Times*

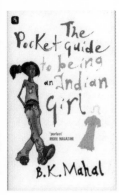

THE POCKET GUIDE TO BEING AN INDIAN GIRL
B.K. Mahal

268pp
ISBN: 1-901969-23-1
RRP £6.99

Born and bred in Dudley, Susham Dillon is a typical teenager – confused, rebellious and going through an identity crisis, stumbling from one social slip to another and confounding social expectations of what it means to be a good Indian girl. In this hugely entertaining guide to life, Susham lays out the rules that make an Indian girl more than just a prospect for another arranged marriage.

'Sparky, funny, touching tale of an Asian teenager' – *The Bookseller*

PADDY INDIAN
Cauvery Madhavan

252pp
ISBN: 101969-04-5
RRP £7.99

When a young Indian doctor arrives in Ireland from an extremely wealthy and westernised medical family in Madras, he finds he is 'just another foreign doctor'. Gradually – and unconsciously – he recreates the lifestyle he is accustomed to in Madras, but finds himself in deep waters when he falls in love with the Professor's daughter . . .

'Cauvery Madhavan is a welcome new voice in contemporary fiction . . . A fine Anglo-Indian comedy of manners and mores' – Liz Thompson, *Publishing News*